HEY KIDS!
You're Cookin' Now!

A Global Awareness Cooking Adventure

by
Dianne Pratt

illustrated by Janet Winter

Acknowledgments

Recipes and other information:
Sarah Lanford, Norberta Butler, Barbara Carey, Robin Pratt, MariLou Conner, Judy Booth, Christine Bird, Carol & Jessica Boudreau, Judith Guilford and the Hancock County Coop. Extension
Art ideas: Sandy Bingham, Robin Pratt and Bobby Pratt
Nutritional Guidance: Beth Davis, Registered Dietician, M.Ed.

Credits

Center Cover Art and Text Art: Janet Winter
Cover Design, Layout and Typesetting: Sherri Eldridge and Dianne Pratt
Cover Border Art: From cotton print used with permission of Alexander Henry Fabrics
Proofreading: G. William Eldridge, Martha Ward, Brenda Koplin, and Fran and Jerry Goldberg
Research and Development Assistance: Robin Pratt and Bobby Pratt

Hey Kids! You're Cookin' Now! A Global Awareness Cooking Adventure
by Dianne Pratt
illustrated by Janet Winter
foreword by Deanna F. Cook
edited by Sherri Eldridge

Published by: Harvest Hill Press
P.O. Box 55, Salisbury Cove, Maine 04672   207-288-8900

First Printing: December 1998

Disclaimer: Childcare givers are strongly cautioned to supervise children in connection with the use and application of information and methods contained in this book. Do not allow children to handle cooking utensils until they are old enough to understand and obey instructions regarding proper use. This book is intended to give accurate information with regard to the subject matter covered. However, the author and publisher accept no responsibility and specifically disclaim any liability, loss, or risk, which is incurred as a consequence, directly or indirectly, from the use and/or application of the contents of this book.

Publisher's Cataloging-in-Publication
Pratt, Dianne M., 1959-

    Hey kids! You're cookin' now! : a global awareness cooking
adventure / by Dianne Pratt ; illustrated by Janet Winter. --
1st ed.
    p. cm.
    Includes index.
    CONTENTS: Recipes for children who are interested in
making breakfasts, breads, lunches, snacks, dinners, desserts,
beverages, and "marvelous mixes." Also includes facts about
diet, nature, and ecology.
    Preassigned LCCN: 98-73980
    ISBN: 1-886862-07-9

    1. Cookery--Juvenile literature. 2. Nature--Miscellaea--Juvenile
literature. 3. Natural foods--Juvenile literature.
I. Winter, Janet, 1926- II. Title.

TX652.5.P73 1998   641.5'123
                        QBI98-1334

Printed in the United States

10% TOTAL RECOVERED FIBER
10% POST-CONSUMER FIBER

DEDICATED TO:

Robin!

Who always <u>knew</u> I could do this, whose enthusiasm for the book kept me going, and whose help in researching, brainstorming and taste testing were invaluable.

and

Bobby!

Who bravely tried new things, contributed his stamp of approval on the kitchen experiments, and whose concern for our world and its animal inhabitants encouraged the global awareness theme.

FOREWORD

Are your kids looking for a fun activity? Invite them into the kitchen to cook up one of the delicious recipes in *Hey Kids! You're Cookin' Now!* As junior chefs flip through the pages, they'll find many enticing recipes, from No Bake Zebra Cake and Bananarama Bread, to Marvelous Macaroni & Cheese and Awesome Applesauce. The nutritious and easy-to-follow recipes are proven winners by the author, Dianne Pratt, and her two kids, Robin and Bobby. Passing the picky eater test, these recipes are easy for little hands to prepare with the help of a parent or teacher.

Playful sidebars take kids one step beyond the recipes - presenting fun facts about food, animals and ecology. (Did you know that in the tropics bananas are dried and ground into flour for baking?) There's even a chapter of Kitchen Crafts and Experiments for crafting recycled paper, making Play Clay, Magic Mud and Acid Rain Test Dip Sticks. The simple ecology-related experiments and kitchen art projects are just right for curious young minds. The book also encourages kids to be good consumers and responsible global citizens.

So turn the page, grab an apron, and start your kids on a cooking adventure! They will all be surprised at how much they'll enjoy learning along the way.

Deanna F. Cook
Senior Editor, *FamilyFun Magazine*
Author of the award-winning book,
The Kids' Multicultural Cookbook

Publisher's Note:

Harvest Hill Press, the publisher of this book, is a Corporate Associate of The Nature Conservancy. Purchase of this book helps make it possible for Harvest Hill Press to annually contribute $1,000 to The Nature Conservancy.

CONTENTS

TOOLS & INGREDIENTS

At the beginning of each recipe and activity are lists of tools and ingredients you will need. Always review these lists first and gather your tools and ingredients before beginning. If you are out of a particular ingredient, check with your adult helper to see if there is a good substitute. Most items can be found in your home, supermarket, backyard or hardware store.

You can adjust some ingredients, like seasonings and sauces, to your personal likes and dislikes. Basic ingredients, such as baking powder or baking soda, require using the exact product and amount specified in the recipe.

Here are a few tools and ingredients you will use in these cooking adventures:

 Wooden spoons won't scratch the bottom of pans and the handles won't get hot.

Oven mitts and pot holders are necessary when handling hot pots, pans and baking sheets.

Use a transparent cup to measure liquids. Look at it from eye level for accurate reading.

 Measuring cups and spoons. Dry ingredients can be measured by filling cups and spoons, then leveling off with a knife.

A cutting board protects countertops. Wash thoroughly before putting away.

Depending on your skill level you can use an electric or hand mixer.

Knives should always be used with adult supervision. Be careful washing them, too.

Mixing bowls come in many sizes. Ingredients blend best when the bowl is not too big or too small.

 Select the size of the saucepan according to the amount of ingredients going into it.

 Canola or olive oil can often be used as a healthier alternative to butter or vegetable oil.

 If fresh is not available, frozen vegetables and fruits are a better choice than canned.

Pasta comes in many shapes and sizes. You can substitute your choice in most recipes.

 Fresh produce in season is economical and packed with vitamins and flavor.

 A rubber spatula is great for getting all of the liquid or batter out of bowls and measuring cups.

 A whisk works great for whipping liquids together.

 Most dairy products are now available in lowfat or nonfat varieties.

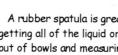 Canned fruits and vegetables are best if packed in water with no added sugar and salt.

 Unbleached all-purpose flour is healthier. Bleached and unbleached all-purpose flours can be used interchangeably.

GETTING READY

Preparation is the secret to being successful at most tasks. This is especially true with cooking. As a well-organized cook you will have more fun, be safe, enjoy better cooking results, and find cleanup to be a breeze!

Here are some tips on where to begin (and end):

-Read BEE SAFE on page 8 and frequently review this information.

-Read the entire recipe and get permission before beginning. If there is a word or procedure you don't understand, check the glossary on page 152 or ask your adult helper to explain.

-Get training from your adult helper before using appliances such as the stove, blender or mixer.

-Put on an apron to protect your clothing. If you have long hair, tie it back so it doesn't get into the food.

-Wash your hands with soap and water.

-Gather all tools and ingredients to be sure you have everything you need for the recipe. If you don't have an ingredient, ask your adult helper if there is something else you might be able to substitute for it.

-As you add each ingredient, set it aside or put it away, so you won't wonder whether you have already added it or not.

-Wipe up spills immediately to save time and "elbow grease" later. Dried-on spills are much harder to clean up.

-When finished, leave the kitchen sparkling clean. Wash the dishes, wipe counter tops and stove, and sweep the floor. Cover and put away all foods. Return all equipment to their proper places.

-HAVE FUN AND TAKE YOUR TIME! Mistakes happen when you are in too much of a hurry. If things don't turn out the way you plan, try again. You can learn a lot from your mistakes.

As you practice your cooking skills, you will discover that good cooks are always learning new things. With experience, you will automatically organize your kitchen projects; but, until then, review this page before beginning any recipe or activity in this book.

"BEE" SAFE

The kitchen is a place of fun activity, but it can also be dangerous. Following some simple rules ensures your safety and enjoyment. To "BEE" SAFE:

- Always ask for permission to use the kitchen and for help if you need it.
- Tie back your hair and make sure your clothing is not loose (roll up sleeves) to prevent getting caught in appliances or being exposed to a hot burner.
- Stay in the kitchen while cooking to keep an eye on things. If you are waiting for something to be done, clean up, or play a game or color at the table.
- Always handle food with clean hands and clean utensils. Wash all surfaces with hot soapy water and rinse thoroughly before and after cooking.
- Always use pot holders to hold pot handles when stirring on the stove, removing items from the stove, and moving things into and out of the oven. NEVER USE A WET POT HOLDER! It won't protect your hands!
- Never let handles stick over the edge of the stove; turn all pot handles toward the center. (Someone might bump into the handle, tip the pot over, and get burned.)
- Do not use spray cooking oil near an oven or stove. Spray pots or pans over the sink.
- When you lift the lid off a pot, first tip up the edge furthest away from you. Otherwise, the hot steam that escapes can burn you.
- Turn off the oven and burners as soon as you finish cooking.

When you see the "Bee" Safe Bee, it is a reminder that your adult helper probably needs to help with that step.

"Bee" Safe Bee

When you see the Mama Bear, discuss the recipe with your adult helper. He or she will know if you have the skills to make the recipe on your own or if adult assistance is needed.

Mama Bear

BREAKFAST & BREADS

PATRIOTIC PANCAKES

Oatmeal Blueberry Pancakes

Makes 12 Pancakes

TOOLS:
medium bowl
hand beater or fork
measuring cups and spoons
non-stick spray cooking oil
frying pan
slotted spatula

INGREDIENTS:
1¼ cups all-purpose flour
¾ cup dry rolled oats
1 cup buttermilk
1 cup 2% lowfat milk
1 tablespoon honey
   or maple syrup
2 eggs
2 tablespoons canola oil
1 tablespoon baking powder
¼ teaspoon salt
½ cup blueberries

Serving: 3 Pancakes	Calories: 354
Protein: 13 gm	Fat: 10 gm
Carbs: 53 gm	Cholesterol: 111 mg
Sodium: 525 mg	Calcium: 241 mg

1. In a medium mixing bowl, beat all ingredients, except blueberries, with hand beater or fork until smooth. (For thinner pancakes add an additional 3 tablespoons milk.)

2. Gently fold in berries.

3. Spray a frying pan with non-stick cooking oil. Heat pan over medium heat just until a few drops of water sprinkled on the pan skitter around.

4. For each pancake, pour about ¼ cup of batter into the hot pan.

5. Cook until pancakes puff up and bubble. (Don't flatten pancakes with your spatula; you want them to be light and fluffy.)

6. Flip pancakes over with the spatula and cook on the other side until light golden brown. (Peek underneath by lifting the edge with your spatula.)

If pancakes are brown on the outside and gooey on the inside, turn down the heat a little bit.

STRAWBERRY SYRUP

Makes 1½ Cups Syrup

TOOLS:
measuring cups and spoons
small saucepan

INGREDIENTS:
½ cup mashed strawberries
1 tablespoon orange juice
1 cup maple syrup

Serving: 6 Tablespoons	Calories: 206
Protein: 0 gm	Fat: 0 gm
Carbs: 53 gm	Cholesterol: 0 mg
Sodium: 8 mg	Calcium: 85 mg

1. Place all ingredients into a small saucepan and simmer 10 minutes over medium heat.

2. Spoon over Patriotic Pancakes, waffles or ice cream!

Animal Fact

In 1782, the American bald eagle was chosen by Congress as the emblem for the United States. Representing strength and courage, it is shown on the national seal holding an olive branch for peace, and arrows for military strength.

APPLE FRENCH TOAST

Serves 4

TOOLS:
pie plate and slotted spatula
fork and bread knife
measuring cups and spoons
non-stick spray cooking oil
non-stick frying pan

INGREDIENTS:
2 eggs
2 egg whites
¼ cup 2% lowfat milk
½ cup apple juice
½ teaspoon vanilla extract
½ teaspoon cinnamon
8 thick slices of bread
canola oil for frying
powdered sugar

Serving: 2 Pieces
Protein: 10 gm
Carbs: 39 gm
Sodium: 288 mg

Calories: 273
Fat: 8 gm
Cholesterol: 107 mg
Calcium: 38 mg

1. Break eggs and egg whites into pie plate. Add milk, apple juice, vanilla and cinnamon. Beat with a fork.

2. Trim crust off bread. Dip slices one at a time into mixture, and soak completely covered for at least 1 minute.

3. Spray frying pan with non-stick oil. Pour 2 teaspoons oil into pan, spread to coat. Place pan on medium burner. Use the spatula to place two soaked slices into the frying pan. Cook on both sides until golden brown. (Use your spatula to peek underneath.) If the French Toast sticks, coat pan with a little more oil for the next batch. Keep warm in the oven until all batches are cooked.

4. Place French Toast on plates, and sprinkle with powdered sugar. Serve with fresh strawberries and *Strappleberry Jam*, page 13.

STRAPPLEBERRY JAM

TOOLS:
tongs
pot of boiling water
three 2-cup lidded containers
potato masher and spoon
measuring cups and spoons
large and small bowls

INGREDIENTS:
3 cups strawberries
1 cup applesauce
1 teaspoon cinnamon
2 pinches ground cloves
3 cups sugar
1 box fruit pectin

Serving: 2 Tablespoons   Calories: 54
Protein: 0 gm   Fat: 0 gm
Carbs: 14 gm   Cholesterol: 0 mg
Sodium: 0 mg   Calcium: 2 mg

Makes 6 Cups Jam

1. Use tongs to briefly dip clean containers and lids in boiling water to sterilize.

2. Wash strawberries, remove stems and thoroughly crush with potato masher. Measure 3 cups mashed strawberries into a large bowl. Add applesauce, cinnamon and cloves.

3. In a small bowl, mix together ¼ cup of the sugar and the box of fruit pectin.

4. Gradually add pectin and sugar mixture to strawberry/applesauce mixture, stirring vigorously. Let stand 30 minutes, but stir every 10 minutes.

5. Gradually mix in remaining sugar. Continue stirring until the sugar is dissolved.

6. Fill containers to about ½ inch from the top. Cover and let stand at room temperature for 24 hours to thicken the jam.

Strappleberry Jam can be kept up to 3 weeks in refrigerator or 1 year in the freezer.

Ecology Fact

Litter can be dangerous to wildlife. Small animals, like mice, climb into bottles only to find they can't get out again. Birds and fish sometimes eat trash thinking it is food. Dispose of litter properly and clean up when others haven't been so thoughtful.

CINNAMON ORANGE SCONES

Makes 8 Scones

TOOLS:

medium mixing bowl
measuring cups and spoons
wooden spoon
grater and fork
pastry cutter or 2 knives
small bowl or cup
pizza cutter or knife
non-stick cookie sheet

INGREDIENTS:

1¼ cups all-purpose flour
⅓ cup sugar
1 tablespoon baking powder
1 teaspoon cinnamon
½ teaspoon salt
1 orange (unpeeled)
⅓ cup lowfat cream cheese
½ cup raisins
1 egg
6 tablespoons buttermilk

Serving: 1 Scone
Protein: 4 gm
Carbs: 32 gm
Sodium: 293 mg

Calories: 171
Fat: 2.5 gm
Cholesterol: 32 mg
Calcium: 99 mg

Preheat oven to 375°.

1. In a medium mixing bowl, combine flour, sugar, baking powder, cinnamon and salt. Stir with spoon until blended.

2. Wash orange and grate its peel.

3. Using pastry cutter or 2 knives, cut cream cheese and grated orange peel into flour mixture.

4. Stir in raisins.

5. In a small bowl, use fork to beat egg with 4 tablespoons of buttermilk.

6. Stir beaten liquid into flour mixture until the dough gathers together into a ball. If needed, add remaining 2 tablespoons of buttermilk.

7. Place the dough ball on a lightly floured surface, lightly dust your hands with flour and knead* the dough about 8 times. Pat out the dough into a circle about 8 inches across and ½ inch thick.

8. With a pizza cutter or knife, cut the dough like a pie into 8 wedges. Place the wedges on a cookie sheet so that they don't touch each other. Bake 12-15 minutes.

* See page 152 for a description of how to knead, or ask for assistance.

Animal Fact

The American alligator spends all of its time in and around the swamps and rivers that are its home. Alligator habitat ranges from North Carolina to Florida, and along the North American Gulf Coast. In some areas where the water level fluctuates, alligators dig a hollow in the mud which fills with water. This guarantees it access to water when the water level drops, and even provides water for other animals. These underground hollows can be up to 65 feet long. The temperature in the hollow remains fairly stable, so the alligator retreats into the hollow to avoid extremes of winter cold and summer heat. The female alligator lays her eggs in a nest made of damp, rotting vegetation and mud. After depositing the eggs, she covers the nest with more vegetation. As the vegetable matter in the nest rots, it gives off heat which helps to incubate the eggs. For the first 6 years of the young alligator's life, it will grow about 12 inches a year!

BREAKFAST BREAD PUDDING

Serves 4

TOOLS:

mixing bowl and whisk
measuring cups and spoons
mixing spoon and knife
8" x 8" baking pan
non-stick spray cooking oil

INGREDIENTS:

2 eggs
¾ cup 2% lowfat milk
1 teaspoon cinnamon
¼ cup sugar
6 slices stale bread
1 apple
½ cup golden raisins

Serving: 1/4 Recipe	Calories: 288
Protein: 8 gm	Fat: 5 gm
Carbs: 55 gm	Cholesterol: 109 mg
Sodium: 251 mg	Calcium: 135 mg

Preheat oven to 350°.

1. In bowl, whisk eggs until fluffy. Beat in milk, cinnamon and sugar.

2. Tear bread into 1-inch chunks. Use spoon to mix bread chunks into egg mixture. Gently stir to coat the bread. Let bread mixture set 15 minutes.

3. Peel, core and dice the apple. Stir diced apple and raisins into the bread mixture.

4. Spray baking pan with non-stick cooking oil. Pour bread mixture into the baking pan. Bake bread pudding 25 minutes, or until top is light golden in color. Spoon into serving bowls.

Serving suggestion:
Top with Pumpkin Sauce, page 17

Animal Fact

You've probably heard the saying, "If you want your plans to run smoothly, you have to get your ducks in a row." But why do the offspring of ducks and geese swim in a row behind their mother? Scientists theorize that ducklings swimming in a row behind mom at regularly spaced intervals conserve their energy. The mother bears the brunt of the work, and the ducklings enjoy reduced drag swimming in her wake. It may also help to keep up with mom who protects them from predators.

PUMPKIN SAUCE

Serves 8

TOOLS:
large bowl and can opener
measuring cups and spoons
hand or electric mixer
saucepan and wooden spoon

INGREDIENTS:
½ cup sugar
2 eggs
2 cups 2% lowfat milk
16-oz. can mashed pumpkin
½ teaspoon ground nutmeg
1 teaspoon vanilla extract

Serving: 1/2 Cup	Calories: 111
Protein: 4 gm	Fat: 2.5 gm
Carbs: 19 gm	Cholesterol: 58 mg
Sodium: 47 mg	Calcium: 89 mg

1. In a large bowl, beat sugar and eggs together with a hand or electric mixer. Stir in remaining ingredients.

2. Pour mixture into a large saucepan. Cook over medium heat, stirring constantly, until the sauce boils. Turn heat to low and continue stirring until the sauce thickens, about 15 minutes.

*Pour warm sauce over
Breakfast Bread Pudding, page 16.
Use extra sauce over vanilla ice cream!*

Food Fact

The original Pilgrim pumpkin pie looked nothing like the one on Grandma's table. After cutting the top off the pumpkin and scraping out the seeds, the Pilgrims filled the pumpkin with apples, sugar, spices and milk. With the top back on, it was baked in the hot ashes of a fire.

TOASTED BAGEL CHIPS

Serves 1

TOOLS:
measuring spoons
cookie sheet
clean spice shaker
knife and pastry brush
non-stick spray cooking oil

INGREDIENTS:
2 teaspoons cinnamon
2 tablespoons sugar
1 plain bagel
¼ cup water

Serving: 1 Recipe	Calories: 304
Protein: 8 gm	Fat: 1.5 gm
Carbs: 67 gm	Cholesterol: 0 mg
Sodium: 381 mg	Calcium: 110 mg

Preheat oven to 350°.

1. Spray cookie sheet with non-stick cooking oil. Combine cinnamon and sugar in spice shaker.

2. Slice bagel into ¼-inch-thick round chips. Use pastry brush to lightly brush chips with water. Generously sprinkle with cinnamon-sugar mixture.

3. Place chips on the cookie sheet in a single layer and bake 5 minutes, or until crispy.

Serve with Fruited Yogurt Dip, page 19.

FRUITED YOGURT DIP

Makes ½ Cup Dip

TOOLS:
measuring cups and spoons
small bowl and mixing spoon

Combine all ingredients. Mix well.
Use Fruited Yogurt Dip with Toasted Bagel Chips or pretzels for a fun snack!

INGREDIENTS:
½ cup plain yogurt
1 tablespoon sugar or honey
¼ teaspoon vanilla extract
2 tablespoons any jam, such as
   Peach Perfect Jam, page 21
  or *Strappleberry Jam*, page 13

Serving: 1/2 Cup
Protein: 7 gm
Carbs: 52 gm
Sodium: 104 mg

Calories: 228
Fat: 0.5 gm
Cholesterol: 2 mg
Calcium: 235 mg

Animal Fact

Rhinoceros are impressive and powerful animals. There are five living species of rhino: White, Black, Indian, Javan and Sumatran. The largest is the White Rhino. The word rhinoceros is made from two ancient Greek words, "rhino" meaning nose and "ceros" meaning horn. Rhinos are the only animals with horns on their noses. Some people think the myth of the unicorn was created when European explorers reported seeing a large horselike animal with a horn on its nose. The greatest threat to the rhino is the illegal poaching for their horns, which are sold for their assumed medicinal value. However, scientific tests have proven that a rhino's horn has no medicinal properties.

HOMESTEAD HARVEST ROLLS

Make these the night before you want them for breakfast.

Makes 12 Rolls

TOOLS:
measuring cups and spoons
small saucepan
large mixing bowl
slightly wet kitchen towel
9" x 13" non-stick pan
non-stick spray cooking oil

INGREDIENTS:
½ cup 2% lowfat milk
1 cup water
¼ cup molasses
¼ cup sugar
2 tablespoons butter
1 teaspoon salt
1 tablespoon dry yeast
1 cup multigrain cereal
   with nuts and dried fruit
¼ cup raisins
3½ cups all-purpose flour

1. In a small saucepan mix together milk, water, molasses, sugar, butter and salt. Stirring constantly, warm over medium heat for 3-4 minutes.

2. Pour warm mixture into large mixing bowl and sprinkle yeast on top. Don't stir! Let sit 10-15 minutes.

3. Stir in cereal and raisins, then mix in flour. Dough should be really stiff.

4. Cover bowl with moistened towel and let dough rise in the bowl until doubled in size, about 45-60 minutes.

5. Spray pan with non-stick cooking oil. With lightly floured hands (dough is very sticky), roll dough into twelve 2-inch balls and place in pan.

6. Cover pan with moistened towel, and let rise again until doubled in size, about 45 minutes.

7. Preheat oven to 350°. Bake *Homestead Harvest Rolls* 20 minutes.

Serve with warm jam. Mmm!

Serving: 1 Roll	Calories: 233
Protein: 5 gm	Fat: 3 gm
Carbs: 46 gm	Cholesterol: 6 mg
Sodium: 240 mg	Calcium: 47 mg

PEACH PERFECT JAM

Makes 6 Cups Jam

TOOLS:
tongs and pot of boiling water
small and large mixing bowls
three 2-cup lidded containers
knife and mixing spoon
potato masher
measuring cups

INGREDIENTS:
2½ pounds ripe peaches
¼ cup lemon juice
3 cups sugar
1 box powdered fruit pectin
1 cup light corn syrup

Serving: 2 Tablespoons	Calories: 80
Protein: 0 gm	Fat: 0 gm
Carbs: 21 gm	Cholesterol: 0 mg
Sodium: 8 mg	Calcium: 2 mg

1. Use tongs to dip containers and lids in boiling water to sterilize.

2. Peel, pit and finely chop peaches. Thoroughly crush peaches with the potato masher. Measure 3¼ cups into large bowl. Add lemon juice.

3. In a small bowl, combine ¼ cup of sugar and the box of fruit pectin.

4. Stirring vigorously, slowly add sugar mixture to peach mixture. Let the mixture rest 30 minutes, but stir it every 10 minutes.

5. Add corn syrup, then gradually stir in remaining sugar. Continue stirring until sugar is dissolved.

6. Fill containers to about ½ inch from the top, cover and let stand at room temperature for 24 hours.

Store 3 weeks in the refrigerator or 1 year in the freezer.

Food Fact

Did you know peach trees are members of the rose family? Maybe that's why peaches smell so good!

BANANARAMA BREAD

What makes this bread especially great is that it is almost completely fat free!   Makes 1 Loaf

TOOLS:
measuring cups and spoons
medium mixing bowl
small bowl and fork
8" x 4" loaf pan
non-stick spray cooking oil
wire cooling rack

INGREDIENTS:
½ cup whole wheat flour
1¼ cups all-purpose flour
½ cup packed brown sugar
2 teaspoons baking powder
½ teaspoon baking soda
¼ teaspoon ground nutmeg
1¼ cups very ripe bananas
½ cup honey
¼ cup 2% lowfat milk

1 Loaf of Bread = 12 Slices

Serving: 1 Slice	Calories: 170
Protein: 3 gm	Fat: 0.5 gm
Carbs: 41 gm	Cholesterol: 0 mg
Sodium: 127 mg	Calcium: 47 mg

Preheat oven to 350°.

1. In a medium mixing bowl, sift together flours, brown sugar, baking powder, baking soda and nutmeg.

2. Use fork to mash bananas in the small bowl. Stir in honey and milk. Add banana mixture to dry mixture, stirring just until slightly moistened.

3. Spray 8" x 4" loaf pan with non-stick cooking oil. Spread banana bread batter evenly in loaf pan.

4. Bake 40-45 minutes. Banana bread is done when a toothpick inserted in the center comes out clean.

5. Use oven mitts to remove pan from oven. Let bread cool in pan 5 minutes, then turn it upside down and give it a gentle shake onto the cooling rack.

Food Fact

Quick bread batter contains baking powder. The baking powder creates carbon dioxide bubbles to make the dough rise. Unlike yeast bread dough, quick breads don't require kneading or rising time. Most quick breads are also sweeter and moister than yeast breads.

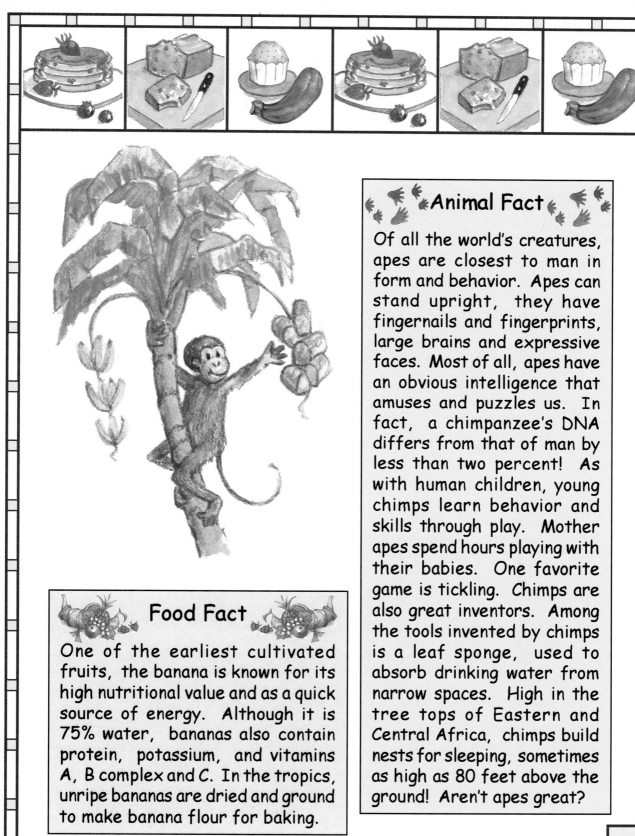

Animal Fact

Of all the world's creatures, apes are closest to man in form and behavior. Apes can stand upright, they have fingernails and fingerprints, large brains and expressive faces. Most of all, apes have an obvious intelligence that amuses and puzzles us. In fact, a chimpanzee's DNA differs from that of man by less than two percent! As with human children, young chimps learn behavior and skills through play. Mother apes spend hours playing with their babies. One favorite game is tickling. Chimps are also great inventors. Among the tools invented by chimps is a leaf sponge, used to absorb drinking water from narrow spaces. High in the tree tops of Eastern and Central Africa, chimps build nests for sleeping, sometimes as high as 80 feet above the ground! Aren't apes great?

Food Fact

One of the earliest cultivated fruits, the banana is known for its high nutritional value and as a quick source of energy. Although it is 75% water, bananas also contain protein, potassium, and vitamins A, B complex and C. In the tropics, unripe bananas are dried and ground to make banana flour for baking.

23

ZUCCHINI MUFFINS

Makes 12 Muffins

TOOLS:
grater
measuring cups and spoons
medium mixing bowl
12-cup muffin tin
non-stick spray cooking oil
   or paper muffin cups

INGREDIENTS:
1 large zucchini
2 eggs
¼ cup canola oil
1½ cups packed brown sugar
½ cup honey
½ teaspoon grated lemon
   peel
2½ cups all-purpose flour
2 tablespoons baking powder
½ teaspoon salt
2 teaspoons cinnamon

Serving: 1 Muffin
Protein: 4 gm
Carbs: 47 gm
Sodium: 119 mg

Calories: 254
Fat: 5.5 gm
Cholesterol: 35 mg
Calcium: 37 mg

Preheat oven to 350°.

1. 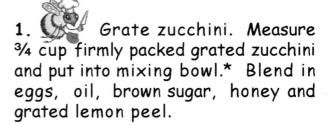 Grate zucchini. Measure ¾ cup firmly packed grated zucchini and put into mixing bowl.* Blend in eggs, oil, brown sugar, honey and grated lemon peel.

2. Add flour, baking powder, salt and cinnamon. Stir just until everything is moist. Do not overmix.

3. Spray muffin tin with non-stick cooking oil. Fill each muffin cup about ¾ full. Bake 15-20 minutes.

You can substitute grated carrots for zucchini, and also add ¼ cup raisins.

Cooking Tip
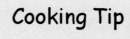
For an easy cleanup, lightly spray grater with non-stick cooking oil.

Ecology Fact

Trees support many kinds of wildlife, add beauty to our homes and provide a cool shady place for sipping lemonade on a hot day. According to a three-year study completed by the U.S. Forest Service in 1995, trees can save millions of dollars in energy and air-pollution costs, too! They improve air quality by removing carbon monoxide, ozone and other pollutants. Trees serve as windbreaks and provide shade for buildings and residences. By blocking winter winds and summer sun, a 25-foot tree on the west side of a typical residence reduces heating and cooling costs by 2-4 percent. Three 25-foot trees along a west wall could cut total home energy costs by as much as 10 percent. That can save as much as $200 per year!

JOHNNY CAKE

Makes 1 Loaf

TOOLS:

measuring cups and spoons
2 medium mixing bowls
whisk or fork
8" round cake pan
non-stick spray cooking oil

INGREDIENTS:

¾ cup cornmeal
1 cup all-purpose flour
1 tablespoon baking powder
½ teaspoon salt
3 tablespoons maple syrup
2 tablespoons canola oil
1 egg
1 cup 2% lowfat milk

Serving: 1 Slice	Calories: 180
Protein: 5 gm	Fat: 5 gm
Carbs: 29 gm	Cholesterol: 29 mg
Sodium: 320 mg	Calcium: 108 mg

Preheat oven to 350°.

1. In a medium mixing bowl, mix together cornmeal, flour, baking powder and salt.

2. In a separate bowl, whisk maple syrup, canola oil, egg and milk. Add to cornmeal/flour mixture, stirring just until everything looks moist.

3. Spray cake pan with non-stick cooking oil. Pour batter into pan and bake for 25 minutes.

4. Use oven mitts to remove the Johnny Cake from oven. Let cool 5 minutes in the pan, then gently flip onto a serving platter. Slice Johnny Cake into 8 wedges like a pie.

Leftover Johnny Cake is great for breakfast with any fruit jam.

Food Fact

Cornmeal was a valuable staple in the diet of early American settlers. When served with beans or legumes it provided needed protein. Cornmeal was commonly made into cornmeal mush, cornbread, puddings and flat bread. The colonists would grind corn into meal by putting corn kernels into a hollow tree stump and pounding them with a heavy log. The young boys were often called on to do this tedious chore.

Helping Hands

Woodlands are important habitats, and are home to many plants and animals. Many wonderful woodland animals lose their homes when trees are cut to make way for roads, factories, farms and expanding towns. There are ways you can help preserve animal habitat:

- Make it a family goal to plant at least one tree a year.

- Join a youth organization that cares for woodlands.

- If your local woodlands are under threat, start a petition with family and friends to ask your town to save them.

- Be informed! Watch and read news stories to increase your awareness of what is going on in your "neck of the woods"!

27

GARDEN VEGETABLE BREAD

Makes 1 Round Loaf

TOOLS:
cutting board
paring knife
frying pan
measuring cups and spoons
large mixing bowl
cookie sheet

INGREDIENTS:
1½ cups peeled and finely
    diced vegetables: onion,
    eggplant, carrot, celery,
    green pepper, zucchini,
    broccoli, mushrooms...
2 tablespoons olive oil
¾ cup very warm water
1 tablespoon sugar
1 tablespoon dry yeast
4 cups all-purpose flour
1 cup whole wheat flour

1 teaspoon salt
½ teaspoon thyme
½ teaspoon tarragon
1½ teaspoons ground dill
¼ cup grated Parmesan
    cheese
1 egg, slightly beaten
2 tablespoons cornmeal

1 Loaf of Bread = 12 Slices
Serving: 1 Slice   Calories: 235
Protein: 8 gm   Fat: 4 gm
Carbs: 42 gm   Cholesterol: 19 mg
Sodium: 235 mg   Calcium: 42 mg

Cooking Tip

To clean up a bowl from batter or dough, immediately fill the bowl
with COLD water and put the spoons and other utensils in it to soak.
Hot water will cook the dough in place, making it difficult to remove.

28

1. 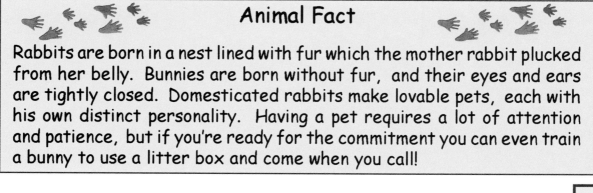 Finely dice your choice of vegetables until you have 1½ cups. Use a tablespoon of olive oil in frying pan to sauté vegetables (except zucchini or eggplant) just until tender, about 2 minutes. Remove from heat and stir in zucchini and eggplant (if you are using them). Set aside to cool.

2. Measure ¾ cup of very warm tap water. Stir in sugar and yeast. Set aside for 5 minutes.

3. While you are waiting for the yeast to activate, combine 2 cups of all-purpose flour, wheat flour, salt, thyme, tarragon, ground dill, Parmesan cheese and egg in a medium mixing bowl.

4. Stir yeast mixture into the dry ingredients. Dough will be stiff.

5. Coat the cooled vegetables with ½ cup all-purpose flour, then gently knead them into the dough. The dough should be slightly sticky; add 2 tablespoons flour if it is very sticky.

6. Brush a large bowl with olive oil and place the dough in the bowl. Brush the top of the dough with remaining olive oil, lightly cover with plastic wrap and let rise until it has doubled in size, about 1 hour.

7. Punch dough down. Sprinkle kneading surface with a little flour, turn dough onto the surface. Knead in enough flour to make the dough soft and no longer sticky. Evenly sprinkle cornmeal on the cookie sheet. Shape dough into a round mound and place on sheet. Cover and let rise 30 minutes.

8. Preheat oven to 350°. Bake 40-50 minutes, or until light golden brown.

Animal Fact

Rabbits are born in a nest lined with fur which the mother rabbit plucked from her belly. Bunnies are born without fur, and their eyes and ears are tightly closed. Domesticated rabbits make lovable pets, each with his own distinct personality. Having a pet requires a lot of attention and patience, but if you're ready for the commitment you can even train a bunny to use a litter box and come when you call!

29

SOFT PRETZELS

Makes 6 Pretzels

TOOLS:
2 medium mixing bowls
measuring cups and spoons
fork
cookie sheet
small dish
pastry brush

INGREDIENTS:
½ cup very warm water
¼ cup honey
1 tablespoon dry yeast
1⅓ cups all-purpose flour
1 teaspoon salt
1 egg yolk
coarse salt

Serving: 1 Pretzel	Calories: 159
Protein: 4 gm	Fat: 1 gm
Carbs: 33 gm	Cholesterol: 36 mg
Sodium: 779 mg	Calcium: 11 mg

Preheat oven to 400°.

1. Measure ½ cup of very warm water into a medium mixing bowl. Dissolve the honey in the water, then stir in the yeast and let it stand 5-6 minutes.

2. In a separate bowl, mix together flour and salt, then stir it into the yeast mixture.

3. On a lightly floured surface, knead pretzel dough 3-4 minutes. If the dough gets really tough, let it rest a couple of minutes, then continue.

4. Divide dough into 6 equal pieces and roll each piece between the palms of your hands to make a "snake."

5. Mold your "snake" like a pretzel or into letter shapes to spell your name. Place on cookie sheet.

6. With a fork, beat egg yolk in a small dish. Brush shaped pretzels with beaten egg yolk and sprinkle with salt (coarse salt if available).

7. Bake 10 minutes or until browned.

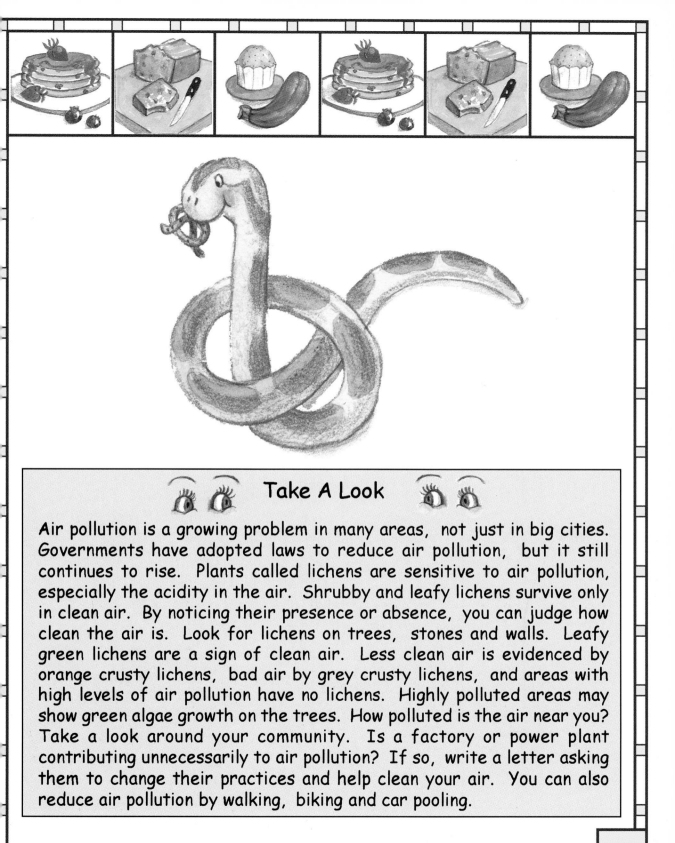

Take A Look

Air pollution is a growing problem in many areas, not just in big cities. Governments have adopted laws to reduce air pollution, but it still continues to rise. Plants called lichens are sensitive to air pollution, especially the acidity in the air. Shrubby and leafy lichens survive only in clean air. By noticing their presence or absence, you can judge how clean the air is. Look for lichens on trees, stones and walls. Leafy green lichens are a sign of clean air. Less clean air is evidenced by orange crusty lichens, bad air by grey crusty lichens, and areas with high levels of air pollution have no lichens. Highly polluted areas may show green algae growth on the trees. How polluted is the air near you? Take a look around your community. Is a factory or power plant contributing unnecessarily to air pollution? If so, write a letter asking them to change their practices and help clean your air. You can also reduce air pollution by walking, biking and car pooling.

FRUITY JUICE CRACKERS

Makes 4 Dozen Crackers

Preheat oven to 375°.

TOOLS:

measuring cups and spoons
mixing bowl
rolling pin and wax paper
knife or cookie cutters
fork
non-stick cookie sheet

INGREDIENTS:

¼ cup canola oil
⅓ cup ginger ale
¾ cup apple juice
1 teaspoon baking powder
⅛ teaspoon cinnamon
3½ cups all-purpose flour

Serving: 3 Crackers	Calories: 137
Protein: 3 gm	Fat: 3.5 gm
Carbs: 23 gm	Cholesterol: 0 mg
Sodium: 41 mg	Calcium: 6 mg

1. In mixing bowl, combine canola oil, ginger ale, juice, baking powder and cinnamon. Stir in flour a little at a time until dough becomes stiff.

2. Use the rolling pin to roll out dough between sheets of wax paper until it is very thin, about ⅛-inch thick.

3. Cut dough into 2-inch squares, or use cookie cutters for fun shapes. Let dough stand for 5 minutes, then prick each cracker several times with a fork.

4. Place crackers on the cookie sheet and bake 5-6 minutes on each side or until golden brown and crisp.

5. Use oven mitts to remove from oven. Cool completely before serving.

Serve with cheese and apple slices.

Cooking Tip

When you need really thin dough roll it between sheets of wax paper. The dough rolls quicker and doesn't require extra flour. Peel away top sheet before cutting cookies or crackers.

32

LUNCH
& SNACKS

See Also: Breaded Vegetables, Chicken and Fish...page 120
Soup Seasoning Mix (Basic Soup)...page 124
Granola...page 114   Salad Dressings...page 123

BROCCOLI CORN CHOWDER

Serves 6

TOOLS:
cutting board and knife
measuring cups and spoons
large saucepan
can opener
mixing spoons

INGREDIENTS:
1 small onion
2 teaspoons butter
1½ cups frozen broccoli
1½ cups frozen corn
17-ounce can creamed corn
1 tablespoon cilantro
1½ cups chicken broth
2 vegetable bouillon cubes
½ cup dry instant mashed
    potato flakes
2 cups 2% lowfat milk
¼ teaspoon pepper

Serving: 1/6 Recipe	Calories: 164
Protein: 8 gm	Fat: 3.5 gm
Carbs: 27 gm	Cholesterol: 10 mg
Sodium: 603 mg	Calcium: 158 mg

1. Chop onion. Melt butter in large saucepan over medium heat, add chopped onion and sauté 1 minute.

2. Add broccoli, frozen and creamed corn, cilantro, broth and bouillon cubes. Cook over medium heat, stirring occasionally, for 10 minutes.

3. Add instant mashed potatoes and milk. Cook about 5 minutes, stirring constantly so milk doesn't scorch.

4. Stir in pepper. Adjust seasonings to taste.

Serve with a crusty bread.

Food Fact

The United States grows more corn than any other country. The top corn-producing states are Iowa and Illinois. Half of the corn grown in the U.S. is used to feed cattle, chickens, sheep and hogs. Did you know corn kernels or cob in some form are found in chewing gum, ketchup, paste, cough syrup, soap, crayons, marshmallows, plastic, printing ink and pancake mix?

34

Take A Look

Before the Europeans settled North America, more than 700 tribes lived on the land that is now the United States. Indians worked hard to meet their basic needs. Women and girls spent many hours gathering wild berries and nuts, and preserving the game meat brought home by the men. Indians were sure to use all parts of the animals they hunted for food, clothing and tools. From carefully tended fields they harvested corn, cooking it into a thick mush or grinding it into flour to make bread. Indian children kept busy learning adult skills, but they also had time for fun. Wrestling and foot races were popular sports and some of the young girls played with corn husk dolls. Native American culture placed great importance on respect for the Earth and nature, with many of their ceremonies honoring nature and the celebration of life. By emulating their respect for our planet, we can make the world a better place.

ALPHABET MINESTRONE

*Leave out the pasta and soup
can be frozen for future use.*

Serves 6

TOOLS:
cutting board
paring knife
measuring cups and spoons
large soup kettle
grater
can opener
wooden spoon

INGREDIENTS:
3 garlic cloves
1 small onion
1 large carrot, peeled
2 stalks celery
1 medium zucchini
½ head small cabbage
1 tablespoon olive oil
1 teaspoon oregano
1 tablespoon basil
¼ teaspoon black pepper
3 vegetable bouillon cubes
3 cups chicken broth

2 cups water
15-ounce can stewed
   tomatoes, with juice
1 cup canned red beans
1 cup dry alphabet pasta

Serving: 1/6 Recipe   Calories: 152
Protein: 7 gm   Fat: 3.5 gm
Carbs: 23 gm   Cholesterol: 1 mg
Sodium: 608 mg   Calcium: 73 mg

1. Peel and finely dice garlic cloves. Separately chop onion, carrot, celery and zucchini into small pieces. Use grater to shred cabbage.

2. Heat olive oil in large soup kettle over medium heat. Add onion and garlic, sauté until soft. Add carrots and celery and cook another 2 minutes. Don't overcook; nobody likes mushy vegetables!

3. Stir in zucchini and cabbage, and cook 2 more minutes.

4. Add oregano, basil and pepper. Reduce heat to low, cook 1 minute.

5. Mix in vegetable bouillon cubes, broth, water and stewed tomatoes. Cover kettle and cook 35 minutes.

6. Turn the heat back up to medium. Add cooked red beans and alphabet pasta. Simmer 8-10 minutes or until pasta is tender, but not mushy.

Serve with Oven-Grilled Cheese Pita, page 40. YUM!

Helping Hands

The three "R's" of recycling are: Reduce, Reuse and Recycle. Reusing items instead of throwing them away limits landfill areas. Here are some fun and functional tips for reusing common waste items.

1) Cereal boxes look great on a bookshelf storing magazines or school papers. Cut off the top at an angle, then wrap the box in newspaper "funnies."

2) Make napkin rings by cutting the "rings" out of cardboard paper towel rolls. Use markers and crayons, or glue on wrapping paper to decorate.

3) For rainy-day fun, use colorful cutouts from product packaging and scraps of aluminum foil for collages, homemade cards and game pieces.

4) Make craft paper from old newspapers; see page 136 for instructions.

5) Make an observation notebook using the back side of used paper. Punch holes and thread ribbon or twine through them to bind your notebook. Decorate the front with pressed leaves and flowers.

TUNA SALAD PICNIC

Serves 6

TOOLS:
small saucepan
knife
cutting board
fork
mixing bowl
measuring spoons

INGREDIENTS:
2 eggs
1 small onion
1 stalk celery
3 6-ounce cans white chunk
  tuna or chicken in water
  (or 1½ cups cooked diced
  tuna or chicken)
¼ cup nonfat mayonnaise
salt and pepper to taste
12 slices whole grain bread
  (try *Garden Vegetable
  Bread*, page 28)

Nutritional Analysis shown using tuna
Serving: 1 Sandwich	Calories: 282
Protein: 33 gm	Fat: 3.5 gm
Carbs: 37 gm	Cholesterol: 96 mg
Sodium: 622 mg	Calcium: 226 mg

1. To hardboil eggs, gently place whole eggs (in shells) in a saucepan and completely cover with cold water. (Cold water takes longer to boil, but the eggs are less likely to crack.) Place on the stove over medium-high heat until the water boils, then turn the heat to low. Simmer eggs 20 minutes.

2. While the eggs are cooking, peel onion. Finely dice onion and celery.

3. When the eggs are done, remove saucepan from stove and flush the pan with cold water until eggs are cool enough to handle. Tap, crack and peel off eggshells. Finely chop eggs.

4. If using canned meat, drain. In the mixing bowl, flake tuna or chicken apart with a fork. Add chopped hardboiled eggs, celery and onion.

5. Toss mixture with a fork until mixed well. Add mayonnaise, salt and pepper to taste. Mix until mayonnaise is evenly blended into tuna or chicken mixture.

6. Spread tuna or chicken salad on bread, cover with another bread slice and diagonally cut into sandwiches.

For your picnic, serve with dill pickles, carrot sticks and Limeade, page 102.

Animal Fact

The polar bear lives in the icy Arctic regions of the North Pole, and the northern coasts of Europe, Asia and North America. It reigns over a world of snow, water and ice where most animals cannot survive. Helping the polar bear to survive this severe climate is its unique hair structure. Although a polar bear looks white, its skin is black and its hair has no color at all! Each hair is really a transparent hollow tube. When sunlight reflects off the hair it makes the bear look white. But, most of the sun's rays pass through the hollow hairs and are trapped by the black skin to warm the bear with solar heat. Adult male polar bears average 1,000 pounds in weight, with paws about 12 inches wide and 18 inches long! Despite their enormous size, polar bears are graceful and athletic. They can jump over cracks in the ice that are more than 20 feet wide, and are excellent long-distance swimmers, often seen several miles from shore. In 1973, the six nations that share the Arctic all signed the Agreement on Conservation of Polar Bears, paving the way to ensure the survival of this majestic animal.

OVEN-GRILLED CHEESE PITA

Serves 4

TOOLS:

measuring cups and spoons
cutting board and knife
mixing bowl and pastry brush
baking sheet

INGREDIENTS:

¼ cup grated cheddar
    cheese
¼ cup grated Monterey
    Jack cheese
¼ teaspoon garlic powder
2 whole wheat pita pockets
½ tablespoon olive oil

Serving: 1/2 Pocket   Calories: 138
Protein: 6 gm   Fat: 5.5 gm
Carbs: 18 gm   Cholesterol: 15 mg
Sodium: 258 mg   Calcium: 105 mg

Preheat oven to 350°.

1. Combine grated cheses in mixing bowl. Sprinkle garlic powder over cheeses and lightly toss mixture.

2. Cut pita pockets in half. Fill halves with 2 tablespoons cheese mixture.

3. Place stuffed pita halves on baking sheet. Using pastry brush, lightly brush tops with olive oil.

4. Place baking sheet in preheated oven. Bake 10 minutes.

5. Use oven mitts to remove baking sheet from oven. Cool 3-5 minutes before eating pitas.

Makes a great addition to a bowl of Alphabet Minestrone, page 36.

Food Fact

Cheese is an excellent source of protein and calcium. It was invented long ago when people discovered how to turn perishable milk into a solid food that would not spoil as quickly. Cheese is produced around the world, mainly from the milk of cows, goats and sheep. The type of milk used, the production method and type of bacteria added to the milk all determine the kind of cheese that will be made. For example, the holes in Swiss cheese are made by bacteria that give off a gas which forms bubbles, or holes, in the cheese as it forms.

Animal Fact

When you think of Australia, what's the first animal that comes to mind? The kangaroo! Kangaroos are the largest marsupials in the world. A marsupial is a mammal with a pouch in which it nurtures and carries its young. Kangaroos live in the hot and dry climate of Australia, and those that live in the desert actually live on less water than camels! If necessary, a kangaroo can go for many weeks without drinking a drop. To keep from losing body fluids, they don't sweat and they rest in shady areas during the heat of the day. Just beneath the surface of their forearms, kangaroos have many tiny blood vessels which they lick and as the moisture evaporates it cools them. A kangaroo's tail is very muscular and is used for balance while hopping.

PARTY PASTA SALAD

You can add anything to this salad, it only gets better!

Serves 6

TOOLS:
measuring cups and spoons
paring knife and grater
medium mixing bowl
strainer
medium saucepan
2 mixing spoons

INGREDIENTS:
1½ cups mixed frozen
   vegetables
1 small carrot, peeled
1 small onion, peeled
1 tablespoon canola oil
2 cups dry rotini pasta
2 tablespoons olive oil
2 teaspoons wine vinegar
1 teaspoon dried basil
1 teaspoon garlic powder
salt and pepper to taste
¼ cup black olives

Serving: 1/6 Recipe
Protein: 7 gm
Carbs: 41 gm
Sodium: 276 mg

Calories: 252
Fat: 7.5 gm
Cholesterol: 0 mg
Calcium: 33 mg

1. Place frozen vegetables in the strainer, and rinse under warm water until thawed. Drain completely, then place in mixing bowl.

2. Grate carrot, chop onion and prepare any other ingredients you want to use. Add to the mixing bowl.

3. Fill medium saucepan ⅔ full with water. Add canola oil and bring to a boil over medium-high heat.

4. Once the water is boiling, add the rotini pasta and stir. When the water boils again, reduce heat to medium. Cook until pasta is tender, about 8-10 minutes.

5. Set strainer in sink. Remove saucepan from stove and carefully pour into strainer to drain pasta.

6. Add pasta to vegetables in mixing bowl and use spoons to toss.

7. Add olive oil, vinegar, spices and black olives. Mix well. Chill 1 hour before serving.

Animal Fact

There are five living subspecies of tiger. The Bengal tiger is the most common, although only 2,500 are left in the wild. The Siberian tiger is the largest, and has very thick fur to survive in the coldest climate. Every tiger has a private hunting territory and several ways of warning other tigers to "stay out"! Tigers mark their territorial borders by scratching trees or leaving a scent. Very few cats like the water, but tigers love it! They often lie in shallow pools to cool off or get away from mosquitoes, or swim and play in the water. Tigers can go days without eating, but when a tiger is hungry it can eat 100 pounds of meat at one sitting! (This is like eating 400 burgers at one meal.) When the tiger is full, it may bury the remaining meat for another meal, or sound out a roar inviting tigers up to a mile away to come share the meal.

CINNAMON TORTILLA CRISPS

Serves 4

TOOLS:
measuring spoons
small empty shaker
cutting board
pastry brush
pizza cutter
cookie sheet

INGREDIENTS:
½ tablespoon cinnamon
2 tablespoons sugar
4 6-inch flour tortillas
1 tablespoon water

Serving: 1 Tortilla
Protein: 3 gm
Carbs: 26 gm
Sodium: 168 mg

Calories: 140
Fat: 2.5 gm
Cholesterol: 0 mg
Calcium: 55 mg

To make regular tortilla chips for dipping in tomato salsa, sprinkle crisps with a small amount of salt instead of cinnamon-sugar mixture.

Preheat oven to 375°.

1. Measure cinnamon and sugar into shaker. Cover holes and shake to blend.

2. Lay out tortillas on the cutting board. Use the pastry brush to lightly brush tortillas with water. Sprinkle each one with cinnamon-sugar mixture.

3. Stack tortillas on top of each other. With the pizza cutter, cut stack into 8 wedges, like a pie.

4. Place tortilla wedges in a single layer on cookie sheet. Place the cookie sheet in the preheated oven and bake 8-9 minutes, or until crisp.

5. Remove from oven with oven mitts and let cool completely before serving with *Fresh Fruit Salsa*, page 45.

Store unused crisps in a sealed plastic or airtight container.

Food Fact

Cinnamon originates in the dried inner bark of a tropical tree. Along with other spices, it was once a valuable source of trade. To discourage competitors from finding their sources, tradesmen often told fantastic tales. One tale was that cinnamon grew in dark forest glens infested with poisonous snakes!

44

FRESH FRUIT SALSA

TOOLS:
paring knife
mixing bowl
measuring cups and spoons

INGREDIENTS:
1 medium apple
8 strawberries
1 kiwi
⅓ cup orange juice
1 tablespoon brown sugar
1 tablespoon honey
2 tablespoons applesauce

Serving: 1/4 Recipe	Calories: 82
Protein: 1 gm	Fat: 0.5 gm
Carbs: 21 gm	Cholesterol: 0 mg
Sodium: 3 mg	Calcium: 17 mg

Serves 4

1. Peel and core apple. Hull strawberries and kiwi by removing leaves and stem base in the fruit. Chop all fruit the size of small peas.

2. In a mixing bowl, stir together the finely chopped fruits. Add orange juice, brown sugar, honey and applesauce. Stir until blended.

Serve with Cinnamon Tortilla Crisps, page 44.

👀 Take A Look 👀

Did you know that over time the "leaves" of cactus adapted to the dry desert climate? They became narrower to conserve moisture and now they are the cactus needles. The needles capture condensation from the fog which drips down to the plant's roots. The sharp edges of the needles also discourage animals from nibbling on the plant's succulent flesh. Now that's nature!

HAWAIIAN STUFFED CELERY

Serves 6

TOOLS:
cutting board
paring knife
measuring cups and spoons
can opener
strainer
medium bowl
rubber spatula
serving plate

INGREDIENTS:
6 long celery stalks
½ cup canned crushed
   pineapple
½ cup lowfat cream cheese,
   softened
1 tablespoon smooth peanut
   butter
1 tablespoon honey
2 tablespoons raisins
2 tablespoons crushed nuts

1. Rinse celery stalks and pat dry with a clean towel.

2. On a cutting board, use the paring knife to trim off the leaves and ends of the celery.

3. Open pineapple and drain in the strainer (save the juice - see Cooking Tip on page 92).

4. In a medium bowl, combine drained pineapple, cream cheese, peanut butter and honey. Stir and mash with rubber spatula until well blended. Stir in raisins.

5. With a table knife, fill the groove of each celery stalk with spread.

6. Sprinkle crushed nuts over celery stalks. Place on a large plate and refrigerate for 30 minutes.

7. Cut each stalk into bite-sized pieces and EAT!

Serving: 1/6 Recipe	Calories: 114
Protein: 4 gm	Fat: 6 gm
Carbs: 12 gm	Cholesterol: 10 mg
Sodium: 148 mg	Calcium: 57 mg

Take A Look

There is a recent approach to forestry that is good news! Forests can receive a certificate stating they are officially "Well Managed." To have a "Well Managed" forest, a landowner must practice forestry management which protects wildlife by creating buffer zones of untouched growth around the forest, and not harvesting the oldest trees. The old-growth trees produce the greatest number of healthy new trees. The landowner must also prove that he pays taxes on time, is a good neighbor and is fair to workers. Once a forest is certified, its owner can place a "Well Managed" label on all wood logged from it. As this practice becomes more widespread, please help sustain the forests by selecting wood with a "Well Managed" label at the lumber yard.

FRUIT SALAD

Serves 3

TOOLS:
paring knife
measuring cups and spoons
2 small bowls
mixing bowl
can opener

INGREDIENTS:
1 apple
20 seedless grapes
1 lemon
½ cup water
1 banana
6-ounce can mandarin
   orange slices
2 tablespoons packed
   brown sugar
2 pinches cinnamon

Serving: 1/3 Recipe   Calories: 147
Protein: 1 gm   Fat: 0.5 gm
Carbs: 37 gm   Cholesterol: 0 mg
Sodium: 8 mg   Calcium: 30 mg

1. Wash apple and grapes and pat dry with a clean towel.

2. Cut lemon in half and squeeze out juice into a small bowl. Add water and stir. (The lemon-water is to dip the fruit in so it won't brown.)

3. Ask an adult to help you cut, core and seed the apple, but do not peel it. Cut apple into bite-sized pieces. Place cut apple in lemon-water.

4. Peel and slice banana into bite-size pieces. Place in lemon-water, then drain off liquid. Place apple and banana pieces into mixing bowl.

5. Drain mandarin oranges and reserve the juice in a small bowl. Add mandarin oranges and grapes to mixing bowl.

6. Mix together brown sugar and the reserved mandarin orange juice. Add cinnamon and stir until the brown sugar dissolves. Pour brown sugar sauce over fruit salad in mixing bowl and lightly toss to coat the fruit.

Fruit Salad is a great snack or addition to any meal.
It also works on top of sherbet!

Animal Fact

The male of the peafowl is called a peacock, the female a peahen. Peafowl belong to the pheasant family and are native to Southeast Asia. Have you heard the expression, "As proud as a peacock"? For his courtship display, the peacock struts his stuff to show off his splendid plumage. He elevates his tail, spreads it like a fan, then rapidly vibrates the tail to make the quills rattle. With his feathers shining in metallic shades of bronze, blue, green and gold, he hopes to impress the peahens with his brilliant performance.

Take A Look

Much of India is a peninsula jutting into the Indian Ocean with the Arabian Sea on the west and the Bay of Bengal on the east. A peninsula is an area of land surrounded on three sides by water. The Indian continent has three distinct regions. In the north are the high peaks of the Himalayas, rising more than 25,000 feet. The Greater Himalayas are the tallest mountain range in the world. South of the mountains are the Northern Plains with very fertile soil from the runoff of the Himalayas. The third region is Peninsular India, a mixture of hills, valleys, jungles and plateaus which form the tip of the peninsula.

CHICK-PEA HUMMUS

Serves 6

TOOLS:
can opener
potato masher
mixing bowl and fork
measuring cups and spoons

INGREDIENTS:
2 15-ounce cans chick-peas
    (garbanzo beans)
¼ cup lemon juice
1 tablespoon olive oil
2 tablespoons plain yogurt
½ teaspoon garlic powder
salt and pepper to taste

1. Open canned chick-peas and drain liquid over sink into a container (save the liquid for a flavorful soup stock).

2. Using potato masher, crush a few chick-peas in the mixing bowl. Slowly add a few more chick-peas and mash. Continue process until all chick-peas are mashed as finely as possible. The texture should be smooth and creamy.

3. Mix in lemon juice, olive oil and yogurt.

4. Add garlic powder, salt and pepper. Stir until dip is well blended.

Serve in a small bowl with wedges of pita bread or crackers.

Serving: 1/6 Recipe
Protein: 7 gm
Carbs: 25 gm
Sodium: 762 mg
Calories: 166
Fat: 5 gm
Cholesterol: 0 mg
Calcium: 65 mg

Helping Hands

Many well-known plants and animals are endangered. Here are some things you can do to protect animals where you live:
1) Don't collect butterflies, wildflowers, or any living thing. Study creatures only in their natural habitat.
2) Keep your dog on a leash if there are nesting birds around.
3) Never buy objects made from ivory, coral, sponges or shells.
4) Respect all living things. Even spiders, moths and ants are a part of the ecological balance.

Animal Fact

One of the strangest mammals on Earth is the duckbill platypus. When the platypus was first discovered, it confused everybody. Scientists didn't know what to make of an animal that had a bill and webbed feet like a duck, a flat tail like a beaver, fur like a mammal, and laid eggs like a reptile! It was eventually placed in a group with only one other animal, the Echidna, or spiny anteater. These two animals are the only mammals that lay eggs. The platypus lives in ponds and streams in eastern Australia. With their sharp claws they dig burrows to live in. For extra protection, a female that is going to have babies builds a very long entrance tunnel to the burrow, up to 100 feet long. A platypus weighs only about 4 pounds, but eats up to 2 pounds of food a day. A single platypus can eat over 12,000 worms a month. Yech!

GRANOLA TRAIL MIX

A take-along snack for hiking, camping and after-school sports.

Serves 6

TOOLS:
measuring cups
small mixing bowl
6 airtight containers or
    airtight sandwich bags

INGREDIENTS:
2 cups granola
    (try *Cruncha Muncha*
    Granola, page 114)
¼ cup peanuts, almonds or
    pecans
½ cup raisins or dates
½ cup dried apricots, apple,
    pineapple, or banana chips
¼ cup mini-chocolate or
    carob chips

Serving: 1/6 Recipe   Calories: 290
Protein: 5 gm   Fat: 10.5 gm
Carbs: 46 gm   Cholesterol: 2 mg
Sodium: 138 mg   Calcium: 43 mg

1.   Combine granola and your choice of other ingredients in mixing bowl.

2.   Spoon equal amounts into 6 airtight containers or zippered sandwich bags.

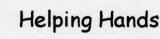 Helping Hands

Hiking can be a pleasant and rewarding activity, a time to put our daily cares behind us, get our blood pumping and renew our commitment to take care of our planet and ourselves. Following a few simple rules of hiking etiquette will protect habitat and show respect for other hikers:

1) Leave nature the way you found it, removing litter along the way. Leave plants and animals in their natural habitat.
2) Keep to the trail so you don't disturb plant and animal life.
3) Keep pets on a leash.
4) Shhh! Be considerate of other hikers who are enjoying the serenity of nature!

Take A Look

Hiking enthusiasts all over the world are familiar with the Appalachian Trail in the eastern United States. Extending from Mount Katahdin in north central Maine to Springer Mountain in northern Georgia, this trail of wild beauty runs 2,050 miles along the crest of the Appalachian Mountains. Passing through 14 states, the trail reaches its peak elevation (6,634 feet) on Clingman's Dome in the Great Smoky Mountains. Completed in 1937, it was designated a scenic trail in 1968. The trail is marked and maintained by hiking groups which are dedicated to its upkeep and preservation.

CRISPY BAKED VEGETABLES

A wonderful appetizer served with
Sweet & Sour Dip, page 55.

Serves 4

TOOLS:

cookie sheet
non-stick spray cooking oil
cutting board and knife
measuring cups and spoons
2 shallow dishes and a fork
tongs or spatula

INGREDIENTS:

2 cups any fresh veggies:
  carrot, zucchini, red or
  green sweet pepper,
  broccoli or cauliflower
1 egg
¼ cup 2% lowfat milk
1 tablespoon canola oil
1 recipe *Shake-It-Up*
  Breading Mix, page 120
2 tablespoons grated
  Parmesan cheese

Serving: 1/4 Recipe
Protein: 9 gm
Carbs: 24 gm
Sodium: 355 mg

Calories: 208
Fat: 8.5 gm
Cholesterol: 61 mg
Calcium: 170 mg

Preheat oven to 450°. Spray cookie sheet with non-stick cooking oil.

1. Cut carrot, zucchini and sweet pepper into ¼-inch strips. Chop broccoli and cauliflower into florets.

2. Beat egg, milk and oil with a fork in a shallow dish. Place *Shake-It-Up Breading Mix* in a separate dish.

3. Dip vegetables into egg mixture, then into the *Shake-It-Up Breading Mix.* Make sure to coat them well. Place on cookie sheet.

4. Repeat step 3 until all vegetables are coated. Bake 5 minutes.

5. Using your oven mitts, remove pan from oven and turn vegetables over with tongs or spatula. Return vegetables to the oven and bake another 5 minutes until vegetables are crisp and tender, and the coating is golden brown. Remove from oven and lightly sprinkle with Parmesan Cheese.

Serve Crispy Baked Vegetables with
Sweet & Sour Dip, page 55.

SWEET & SOUR DIP

Serves 4

TOOLS:
measuring cups and spoons
small saucepan and spoon
small dipping dishes

INGREDIENTS:
⅓ cup packed brown sugar
½ cup pineapple juice
2 teaspoons vinegar
1 tablespoon cornstarch
1 tablespoon soy sauce

Nutritional Analysis for Dip only

Serving: 1/4 Recipe	Calories: 96
Protein: 0 gm	Fat: 0 gm
Carbs: 24 gm	Cholesterol: 0 mg
Sodium: 265 mg	Calcium: 22 mg

1. Combine all ingredients in saucepan. Use the wooden spoon to stir until cornstarch is completely dissolved.

2. Place saucepan on stove over medium heat. Stirring constantly, bring to a boil. (Stir constantly, or the sauce will clump up!)

3. Boil 1 minute until mixture thickens and begins to look more clear than milky.

4. Spoon into dipping dishes. Allow to cool 5 minutes before serving.

To Make Sweet & Sour Chicken: Make a double recipe of *Sweet & Sour Dip*. In a large skillet combine *Sweet & Sour Dip* with 1½ cups cooked diced chicken, a small chopped onion, a small chopped green pepper, drained 15 oz. can pineapple chunks, and ¼ cup chopped maraschino cherries. Simmer over medium heat 15-20 minutes, until onion is clear. Serve over cooked rice.

Food Fact
Brown sugar contains molasses and, unlike white sugar, it contains trace amounts of calcium, iron and potassium.

AWESOME APPLESAUCE

Oh, so much better than store bought!   *Serves 4*

TOOLS:
measuring cups and spoons
paring knife
medium saucepan
potato masher or fork

INGREDIENTS:

6 medium McIntosh or
    Red Delicious apples
⅓ cup packed brown sugar
1 teaspoon cinnamon
1 cup water

Serving: 1/4 Recipe	Calories: 180
Protein: 0 gm	Fat: 0.5 gm
Carbs: 47 gm	Cholesterol: 0 mg
Sodium: 9 mg	Calcium: 32 mg

1. Peel apples, then core and cut into quarters.

2. Put cut apples, brown sugar, cinnamon and water into saucepan. Cover and simmer on medium heat for 15-20 minutes.

3. Allow the apples to cool completely, then mash with a potato masher to desired smoothness.

Experiment with different kinds of apples to discover which you prefer. Each variety has a unique cooking consistency, flavor and sweetness.

Food Fact

The sweet-smelling blossoms make it easy to understand that apple trees are related to the rose family. There are actually thousands of varieties of apples. An apple's variety determines if it is good for eating, cooking, cider or canning.

DINNER
& VEGETABLES

SPAGHETTI SQUIGGLES

Serves 4

TOOLS:
cutting board and knife
measuring cups and spoons
large frying pan
can opener
wooden spoon

SAUCE INGREDIENTS:
1 small onion
1 small green pepper
8 medium mushrooms
2 tablespoons olive oil
¼ cup water
¼ cup *Spaghetti Sauce
    Seasoning* mix, page 119
6-ounce can tomato paste
1 cup water
15-ounce can crushed
    tomatoes
1 teaspoon honey

Nutritional Analysis for Sauce only
Serving: 1/4 Recipe   Calories: 149
Protein: 5 gm   Fat: 7 gm
Carbs: 19 gm   Cholesterol: 0 mg
Sodium: 585 mg   Calcium: 80 mg

1.   Ask an adult to peel onion. Dice onion, pepper and mushrooms.

2.   In a large frying pan over medium-high heat, sauté vegetables in olive oil 5 minutes. Blend in water and *Spaghetti Sauce Seasoning* mix.

3. Over medium heat, stir with the wooden spoon for 1 minute.

4. Add remaining ingredients. Turn heat to low. Simmer sauce uncovered for 40 minutes, stirring occasionally.

5. While sauce is simmering, prepare spaghetti noodles or other pasta, see facing page.

Serve hot sauce over prepared spaghetti or other pasta.

Food Fact

Pasta was introduced into the New World by early European settlers. In 1786, Thomas Jefferson brought a die (a special plate for cutting pasta) back from Italy so he could make pasta for his friends. Pasta later became popular in the United States after the large Italian immigration in the 1800's.

To Prepare Pasta:
TOOLS:
measuring cups and spoons
large pot
wooden spoon and strainer
INGREDIENTS:
4 cups water
1 tablespoon olive oil
¼ teaspoon salt
½ of a 16-ounce box
    spaghetti or other pasta

Nutritional Analysis for Pasta only
Serving: 1/4 Recipe   Calories: 216
Protein: 7 gm   Fat: 1.5 gm
Carbs: 42 gm   Cholesterol: 0 mg
Sodium: 151 mg   Calcium: 11 mg

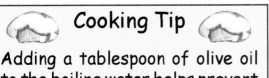

Cooking Tip

Adding a tablespoon of olive oil to the boiling water helps prevent pasta from sticking together.

Serves 4

1. Measure water, oil and salt into pot. Place on stove over high heat until water boils.

2. Holding spaghetti over pot, break in half and drop gently into boiling water. Be careful not to splash, the water is very hot! Bring to a boil. Reduce heat to medium and simmer 10 minutes or until tender. Stir often to prevent spaghetti from sticking together.

3. When spaghetti is done, place strainer in the sink. Using oven mitts, carefully tip the pot away from you and pour spaghetti into the strainer. Shake strainer to drain water.

Top with Spaghetti Sauce, page 58.

POCKET PIZZA

Serves 4

TOOLS:
non-stick spray cooking oil
2 cookie sheets
rolling pin
pastry brush
measuring cups and spoons
fork

INGREDIENTS:
pizza dough, page 61 or 113
1 tablespoon olive oil

Topping:
½ cup pizza sauce
1 cup shredded
    Mozzarella cheese
1 cup chopped veggies:
    mushrooms, onion,
    green pepper, spinach,
    asparagus, olives...

Nutritional Analysis includes
Can't Wait Pizza Dough, page 61
Serving: 1/4 Recipe   Calories: 401
Protein: 17 gm   Fat: 15.5 gm
Carbs: 52 gm   Cholesterol: 18 mg
Sodium: 736 mg   Calcium: 362 mg

Preheat oven to 400°.

1. Spray cookie sheets with non-stick cooking oil.

2. Divide pizza dough into 4 equal parts. Use the rolling pin to roll each piece into a 9-inch circle.

3. Place dough on cookie sheets and brush with a thin layer of olive oil.

4. Layer a quarter of the ingredients on half of each circle, leaving a half-inch space around the edge. Wet your finger and moisten the half-inch space around the edge, then fold dough over filling. Pinch the edges together to seal. Poke holes in the top of each *Pocket Pizza* with a fork. Bake 15 minutes, or until golden brown.

Take A Look

In the Southern Hemisphere, and almost halfway around the world from England, its mother country, lies Australia, also called "the land down-under." "Australia" means "unknown southern land" and early maps often confused it with Antarctica. Australia is home to marsupial animals, including kangaroos, wallabies and wallaroos.

60

CAN'T WAIT PIZZA DOUGH

This dough can be used right away without waiting for it to rise!

Serves 4

TOOLS:
mixing bowl and sifter
measuring cups and spoons
fork

INGREDIENTS:
1 cup all-purpose flour
1 cup whole wheat flour
½ teaspoon salt
2 teaspoons baking powder
⅔ cup 2% lowfat milk
1 tablespoon olive oil

Serving: 1/4 Recipe
Protein: 9 gm
Carbs: 47 gm
Sodium: 513 mg

Calories: 265
Fat: 5 gm
Cholesterol: 3 mg
Calcium: 145 mg

1. Sift together flours, salt and baking powder.

2. Using a fork, stir in the milk and olive oil until the dry ingredients are moist and dough forms.

3. Gather dough into a ball. On a lightly floured surface, knead dough for 10 minutes. Cover and let it rest for 5 minutes. Now you are ready to make *Pocket Pizza,* page 60.

Yeast dough takes longer but is definitely worth it!
See page 113 for recipe.

61

BAKED FISH STICKS
or
CHUNKY CHICKEN BITS

Serves 4

TOOLS:

non-stick spray cooking oil
9" x 13" baking dish
dish towel
cutting board and knife
pie plate
whisk or fork

INGREDIENTS:

1 tablespoon canola oil
1 pound white fish fillets
    (flounder, cod...) *or*
    1 pound fresh chicken
    breast fillets
¼ teaspoon salt
1 recipe *Shake-It-Up*
    Breading Mix, page 120
1 teaspoon grated lemon rind
1 egg
1 egg white
¼ cup 2% lowfat milk

Preheat oven to 400°. Spray baking dish with non-stick cooking oil, then coat with canola oil.

1. Rinse fish or chicken fillets. Pat dry with a clean dish towel. Lightly sprinkle salt on both sides of fillets.

2. For fish sticks, carefully cut fillets into long strips. For chicken bits, cut fillets into 1 inch squares.

3. Place *Shake-It-Up Breading Mix* and grated lemon rind into a small paper bag. In the pie plate, add egg, egg white and milk, then beat with a whisk or fork until egg is well blended.

4. Dip fish or chicken pieces into the egg and milk mixture. Place fish or chicken pieces, a few at a time, into bag, hold bag closed and shake well.

5. Place coated fish sticks or chicken bits on baking dish. Bake until golden brown, about 12-15 minutes. Use oven mitts to remove dish from oven.

Serve Baked Fish Sticks with Quick & Easy Tartar Sauce, page 63.

Serving: 1/4 Recipe	Calories: 310
Protein: 35 gm	Fat: 9.5 gm
Carbs: 19 gm	Cholesterol: 136 mg
Sodium: 575 mg	Calcium: 136 mg

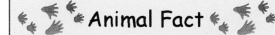
QUICK & EASY TARTAR SAUCE

Makes ¾ Cup Sauce

TOOLS:
small bowl
measuring cups and spoons
fork

INGREDIENTS:
½ cup nonfat mayonnaise
¼ cup sweet relish
1 tablespoon lemon juice

Measure all ingredients into bowl. Blend well with a fork.

Store unused tartar sauce in a small jar or container in the refrigerator for up to 2 weeks.

Serving: 3 Tablespoons	Calories: 22
Protein: 0 gm	Fat: 0 gm
Carbs: 5 gm	Cholesterol: 0 mg
Sodium: 218 mg	Calcium: 0 mg

63

TWICE-BAKED POTATOES

Serves 4

TOOLS:
fork
wire rack
measuring cups
knife
spoon
medium mixing bowl
potato masher
8" x 8" baking pan

INGREDIENTS:
4 large baking potatoes
¾ cup grated cheddar
   cheese
½ cup 2% lowfat milk
salt and pepper to taste
½ cup chopped frozen
   broccoli

Serving: 2 Potato Halves   Calories: 250
Protein: 9 gm   Fat: 7.5 gm
Carbs: 37 gm   Cholesterol: 25 mg
Sodium: 439 mg   Calcium: 208 mg

Preheat oven to 350°.

1. Scrub potatoes and prick holes in them with the fork. Place potatoes on oven rack. Bake 45-60 minutes.

2. Use oven mitts to remove potatoes from oven. Cool on wire rack.

3. When potatoes are cool enough to handle, cut in half lengthwise. Use a spoon to scoop potato flesh out of the skins and place in mixing bowl. Reserve the potato skins for stuffing.

4. Use the potato masher to mash potato flesh in the bowl. Add ½ cup of the grated cheddar cheese, milk and salt and pepper to the mashed potatoes. Combine ingredients by mashing with potato masher until mixture is well blended and fluffy. Stir in chopped broccoli.

5. Spoon the potato-cheese mixture back into the reserved potato skins.

6. Place stuffed potatoes in baking pan. Sprinkle with remaining cheese.

7. Bake 15 minutes.

Experiment by using different chopped vegetables and cheeses.

Ecology Fact

Most of the Sahara Desert in northern Africa receives less than 5 inches of rain per year, and parts of the desert have no rainfall for years! The Sahara is the largest desert on Earth. It spans an area of over 3 million square miles, from the Atlantic Ocean on the east to the Red Sea on the west. Very little vegetation grows in the Sahara, but around its borders are grasslands. The grasslands naturally regenerate themselves and keep the desert from expanding. Lately, overgrazing by cattle and the removal of timber from the grasslands is causing the Sahara Desert to expand southwards at a rate of 30 miles a year. Conservationists are working with the people of the South Sahara to preserve these grasslands for the many species of plants and animals living there.

VEGGIE-RICE BURGERS

Serves 4

TOOLS:
grater
measuring cups and spoons
medium mixing bowl
non-stick spray cooking oil
frying pan and spatula

INGREDIENTS:
1 carrot
1 stalk celery
1½ cups cooked brown rice
¼ cup fresh chopped
   parsley
1 teaspoon salt
½ teaspoon black pepper
1 tablespoon minced
   dried onion
½ teaspoon garlic powder
¼ cup cornmeal
⅓ cup whole wheat flour
2 eggs
2 teaspoons canola oil

1. Grate carrot and celery.

2. Stir together all ingredients in mixing bowl. For easier handling, cover and refrigerate for 30 minutes.

3. Shape into four ½-inch-thick patties.

4. Spray frying pan with non-stick cooking oil, then place on medium heat.

5. Cook patties 6 minutes, flip with spatula and cook 5 minutes more.

Serve burgers on rolls with lettuce, tomato, onion, catsup, mustard, pickles, relish, etc.

Serving: 1 Burger	Calories: 219
Protein: 8 gm	Fat: 6 gm
Carbs: 35 gm	Cholesterol: 106 mg
Sodium: 637 mg	Calcium: 46 mg

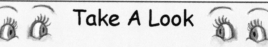

Take A Look

Bamboo plants are important to the economy of several regions. Bamboo is used for food, building houses, furniture, plumbing, baskets and musical instruments. Each plant sends up many shoots from its roots. During a lifetime of over 100 years, most bamboo plants produce seeds only once. Pandas live in the bamboo forests and need to eat large amounts of bamboo every day. Although bamboo grows rapidly, so much is harvested that pandas are now an endangered species.

Animal Fact

The giant panda is so rare today that there are less than 1,000 in the entire world. Seen in the wild only in the mountains of central China and eastern Tibet, pandas are listed as an endangered species. Giant pandas live alone in the bamboo forests. They are mainly ground dwellers, finding shelter in caves, hollow trees or rock crevices, but they will also climb trees to escape danger. Giant pandas feed on bamboo shoots and roots, and have special thumblike structures on their front paws to grasp the bamboo's slender stems. Conservation efforts are now helping to protect the giant panda and the bamboo forests.

CHA-CHA CHILI

Serves 4

TOOLS:

large covered saucepan or
    crockpot
can opener
measuring cups and spoons
cutting board and knife

INGREDIENTS:

16-ounce can sliced
    tomatoes and their juices
16-ounce can crushed
    tomatoes
1½ cups cooked canned red
    kidney beans
1 cup corn, fresh or frozen
1 medium onion
1 small zucchini
1 small green pepper
1½ tablespoons *Chili*
    Seasoning Mix, page 118
¼ cup warm water

Serving: 1/4 Recipe	Calories: 203
Protein: 10 gm	Fat: 1 gm
Carbs: 41 gm	Cholesterol: 0 mg
Sodium: 613 mg	Calcium: 93 mg

1. Open the cans of tomatoes and kidney beans. Pour contents, including liquids, into saucepan or crockpot. Add corn. Place on burner over medium heat.

2. Peel and chop onion. Chop zucchini and pepper. Add vegetables to the saucepan.

3. Mix ¼ cup dry *Chili Seasoning Mix* with ¼ cup warm water. Stir into chili.

4. Raise heat to medium-high until chili boils. Cover, reduce heat to low and simmer 30 minutes.

Serve with hot rice,
Bread Sticks, page 113,
or Johnny Cake, page 26.

Food Fact

Beans are a good nutritional food, not just occasionally, but as regular daily fare. They are inexpensive, versatile and pack lots of nutritional value into a tiny package. A cup of cooked beans has 35 to 40 grams of complex carbohydrates and 15 grams of protein. Beans are high in calcium, potassium, iron, B vitamins and fiber, yet contain only a trace of fat!

Animal Fact

A parrot's plumage is made for living in a tropical forest. There are many brightly colored leaves, flowers and fruits in tropical forests. The parrots' colors blend in with the colorful forests and actually help hide them from predators. Every parrot species in the world has its own special colors, and each parrot can tell if another parrot is a member of its species just by looking at it. Male and female parrots almost always live together in pairs and are very affectionate. They are often seen sitting together, rubbing their bills and preening each other's feathers. Parrots are very good parents, too. While most bird parents push their young out of the nest as soon as possible, parrots allow their young to stay around (and be fed) for a long time. Wild parrots belong in the wild, as do all wild animals. Please help parrots by refusing to buy birds taken from the wild and ask your friends to do the same.

SWEET POTATO OVEN FRIES

Serves 4

TOOLS:

non-stick spray cooking oil
vegetable scrub brush
knife and cutting board
large mixing bowl
non-stick cookie sheet

INGREDIENTS:

3 large sweet potatoes
1 tablespoon canola oil
1 teaspoon salt

Serving: 1/4 Recipe	Calories: 267
Protein: 3 gm	Fat: 3.5 gm
Carbs: 56 gm	Cholesterol: 0 mg
Sodium: 598 mg	Calcium: 29 mg

Preheat oven to 425°.

1. Spray cookie sheet with non-stick cooking oil.

2. Use the vegetable scrub brush to scrub sweet potatoes.

3. Sweet potatoes are very hard, so ask an adult to cut them. Cut lengthwise into ½-inch-thick strips.

4. Place potato strips in the mixing bowl. Add oil and salt, stirring to coat.

5. Spread strips in a single layer on cookie sheet. Bake 30 minutes, or until potatoes are a light crispy brown.

Food Fact

Sweet potatoes can have red, yellow, white or brown skin. Their flesh (pulp) can be orange, yellow, red or purple. Native to the New World tropics, sweet potatoes are highly prized in southern cooking. The root of a trailing vine in the morning glory family, sweet potatoes are high in vitamin A. They are also known for their value in replenishing the fertility of soil. In other words, sweet potato scraps are "gold" for your compost!

Ecology Fact

People often think of wetlands as wasted space that could be used for something better. However, wetlands are the feeding and breeding grounds of many animals, and home to diverse species of plant life. Destroying wetlands reduces wildlife and increases the risk of flooding. Here are some wetland facts of interest:

- 75% of commercially harvested fish and shellfish rely on wetlands for at least a part of their life cycle.
- 43% of the 595 plant and animal species listed as threatened or endangered depend on wetlands for their survival.
- 75% of all waterfowl breed only in wetlands.
- In 1780, there were about 221 million acres of wetlands in the U.S. Today, we have less than 99 million wetland acres.

For a close-up look at wetlands, make a mini-wetland terrarium in a large fish bowl. Your library will have the information you need.

CHICKEN STIR-FRY

Serves 4

TOOLS:

measuring cups and spoons
cutting board and knife
small bowl
wok or large fry pan
large slotted spoon
oven mitts and wooden spoon

INGREDIENTS:

2 tablespoons soy sauce
1 tablespoon honey
1 tablespoon lemon juice
¼ teaspoon ground ginger
2 teaspoons canola oil
1 teaspoon sesame oil
1¼ cups cubed chicken
¾ cup chopped carrots
¾ cup chopped broccoli
¾ cup chopped green pepper
¾ cup snow peas
1 small onion, chopped
4 cups cooked rice

1. If using frozen vegetables, thaw, then pat dry with a towel.

2. In small bowl, stir together soy sauce, honey, lemon juice and ginger.

3. Put oils in wok. Place wok over medium-high heat, warm 1 minute.

4. Place chicken in large slotted spoon and hold handle of wok with pot holder in the other hand. Carefully lower chicken into wok, taking care not to get burned. Stir-fry chicken until it is no longer pink in the center (about 2 minutes). Use the same careful method to add carrots into the wok. Stir-fry 1 minute. Again, use the same method to carefully add remaining vegetables into the wok. Stir-fry 2 minutes. (Cooking time will be less if using pre-cooked veggies.)

5. Add soy sauce mixture. Cook 1 minute more, stirring constantly. Vegetables should be cooked through, but still slightly crisp when done.

Serve at once over cooked rice.

Serving: 1/4 Recipe
Protein: 23 gm
Carbs: 59 gm
Sodium: 133 mg

Calories: 390
Fat: 6.5 gm
Cholesterol: 45 mg
Calcium: 84 mg

Food Fact

The stir-fry method of cooking originated long ago in China during a long period of fuel shortages. To cook a meal using the least amount of tinder for the cooking fire, Chinese cooks spent a lot of time preparing ingredients in advance. They chopped and chopped until the food was in very small pieces, which reduced its cooking time to under 2 minutes. The primary cooking utensil was the wok. The wok is a thin metal bowl that sits on a base. It is placed over the heat source and quickly and evenly conducts the heat. In addition to stir-frying, woks are used for deep-fat frying, braising and even steaming when used with a bamboo basket. You can conserve energy by stir-frying food as the Chinese do. Stir-fried foods retain more color, flavor and nutrients, too!

TACO SALAD BOWLS

Serves 6

TOOLS:

pastry brush
can opener and muffin tin
saucepan and wooden spoon
cutting board and knife
measuring cups and spoons
non-stick spray cooking oil

INGREDIENTS:

6 6-inch soft corn tortillas
1 small onion
1 small zucchini
2 tomatoes
½ small head lettuce
16-ounce can refried beans
1 tablespoon *Chili
    Seasoning Mix*, page 118
2 tablespoons cornmeal
¼ cup grated Monterey
    Jack cheese
6 tablespoons sour cream
6 tablespoons salsa

Serving: 1 Taco Bowl
Protein: 10 gm
Carbs: 34 gm
Sodium: 498 mg

Calories: 202
Fat: 5.5 gm
Cholesterol: 10 mg
Calcium: 143 mg

Preheat oven to 400°.

1. Lightly brush both sides of tortillas with water. To make the tortilla shell bowl, line each of 6 muffin cups with a tortilla, making folds or pleats in the tortilla as needed. Bake 5-8 minutes or until tortillas are light golden brown.

2. Remove from oven, and cool shells in muffin tin for 5 minutes.

3. Finely and separately chop onion, zucchini and tomatoes. Cut lettuce into shreds.

4. Spray saucepan with non-stick cooking oil. Sauté onion and zucchini in saucepan for 2 minutes, then stir in refried beans and *Chili Seasoning Mix*. Heat thoroughly over medium heat for 4 minutes.

5. Remove from heat and stir in cornmeal. Let mixture sit 2 minutes, then divide it evenly into each of the 6 tortilla bowls.

6. Top *Taco Salad Bowls* with shredded lettuce and chopped tomato. Sprinkle with cheese, add a dollop of sour cream and salsa. Olé!

Take A Look

The wonders of the Earth don't end on its surface. Underground are caverns that have been forming for millions of years, providing some of the Earth's most spectacular landscapes. One of the largest and most famous is Carlsbad Caverns in the Guadalupe Mountains of southeastern New Mexico. They are among the oldest caverns in the world, with 30 miles of surveyed corridors, and there are still areas yet to be explored. The cavern was created when bubbling ground water slowly eroded the inside of the porous limestone mountain. In the process, crystal-clear pools, huge chambers, and canyon-like passages with stalactite and stalagmite columns were formed. A stalagmite is a cone-shaped mineral deposit rising up from the cavern floor. A stalactite is the same as a stalagmite but it hangs down from the cavern ceiling. They are both formed by the dripping of mineral rich water that solidifies and builds up over time. Stalagmites and stalactites often meet in the middle to form grand displays of floor to ceiling pillars. Many caverns, including the Carlsbad Caverns, are open to public touring. Don't miss these awe-inspiring wonders!

SALAD TOSS

Serves 6

TOOLS:
clean dry dish towel
large salad bowl
vegetable scrub brush
cutting board and knife
vegetable peeler
grater

INGREDIENTS:
1 small head lettuce
   or other salad greens
1 small cucumber
2 tomatoes
1 large carrot
your choice of celery,
   mushrooms, green onion,
   cauliflower, broccoli,
   radishes, sweet red or
   green peppers, olives...

Serving: 1/6 Recipe
Protein: 2 gm
Carbs: 6 gm
Sodium: 89 mg

Calories: 36
Fat: 1 gm
Cholesterol: 0 mg
Calcium: 35 mg

1. Choose as many different salad greens as you like and wash them under cold water. Pat dry with towel.

2. Remove any bruised or discolored greens and put waste in the compost. (Learn about composting with the *Heap O' Compost*, page 134.)

3. Gently tear greens into bite-sized pieces and place in the salad bowl.

4. With a vegetable brush, scrub cucumber, tomatoes, carrot and your other vegetables.

5. Using vegetable peeler, peel then grate carrot. Cut other vegetables into slices, wedges and chunks and add to the salad bowl.

6. Cover salad bowl and refrigerate until ready to serve.

Serve with purchased dressing or prepare your favorite from the Basic Dressing Mix, page 122.

Take A Look

Serengeti National Park is a wildlife refuge in northern Tanzania, East Africa. Established in 1951, it is a major tourist attraction. The park covers an area of over 15,000 square miles, offering protected habitat to black rhinos, lions, leopards, gazelles, zebras and giraffes.

Animal Fact

Giraffes are the tallest land animal. Their great height comes from their long necks and legs, allowing them to reach leaves high in the trees. Their long legs make huge steps when they walk or run. If you went for a walk with a giraffe, you would have to run as fast as you can just to keep up with a giraffe's slow gait. A walking giraffe takes strides 15 feet long! Although they have few enemies and appear docile, giraffes are fully equipped to defend themselves. A mother giraffe will fight a predator with powerful kicks from her front and rear legs. But, given a choice, giraffes prefer to walk (or run) from trouble. It wasn't the giraffe's height, but its speed, that gave it its name. The word "giraffe" comes from an Arabic word *xirapha*, meaning "the one that walks very fast."

MARVELOUS MACARONI & CHEESE

Serves 6

TOOLS:

2-quart casserole dish
measuring cups and spoons
medium saucepan
strainer and grater
small bowl and fork

INGREDIENTS:

2 cups uncooked macaroni
1 egg
8 ounces grated lowfat
   cheddar cheese
1 cup skim milk ricotta
   cheese
½ cup sour cream
½ cup 2% lowfat milk
½ teaspoon salt
¼ teaspoon pepper
¼ cup dry breadcrumbs
¼ teaspoon paprika
1 teaspoon butter

Preheat oven to 350°. Spray casserole dish with non-stick oil.

1. In a saucepan, boil macaroni according to package instructions. Drain macaroni in strainer.

2. In small bowl, beat egg with fork.

3. In 2-quart casserole dish, combine egg, cheeses, sour cream, milk, salt and pepper. Stir in drained macaroni.

4. Sprinkle casserole with breadcrumbs and paprika. Dot with bits of butter. Cover and bake 30 minutes. Uncover, bake 5 minutes more.

Serve with Salad Toss, page 76.

Serving: 1/6 Recipe	Calories: 379
Protein: 27 gm	Fat: 12 gm
Carbs: 42 gm	Cholesterol: 66 mg
Sodium: 456 mg	Calcium: 645 mg

Animal Fact

Almost every animal has a way to defend itself. Animal claws and teeth make excellent weapons. But, some animals simply rely on speed to escape. Others puff up their bodies or fluff up their fur to make themselves look larger and more frightening. The armadillo has thick armor-like skin and when it rolls up into a ball, it is completely covered with "armor."

Ecology Fact

A habitat is the natural home of a group of plants or animals. Try to find different habitats in your area. You shouldn't have much trouble locating one, even in your own back yard! Look around trees, under rocks and in the garden. Is there a pond nearby? Ponds are home to a large community of different plants and animals. For a fun habitat experiment, gather four chopsticks or four 10-inch-long sticks, 5 feet of string or twine, a ruler, and a hammer or rock. Now find a spot that is out of the way from where you usually walk. Measure an area that is 1 foot by 1 foot square, and hammer a stick about 4 inches into the ground on each of the four corners. Wrap the string around the 4 corner "posts" and tie it in a knot. This is your observation area. Take a close look, use a magnifying glass if you have one. Over the next few days write down everything you see in the observation area, and make a map of where you found it. How many different plants, animals, and insects belong to this particular habitat? How can you protect them in their natural habitat?

BUNNY'S BEST SLAW

A wonderful healthy anytime snack!   Serves 4

TOOLS:
2 mixing bowls
grater
mixing spoon
measuring cups and spoons

INGREDIENTS:
2 large carrots, peeled
1 apple, peeled
⅓ cup raisins
2 teaspoons lemon juice
2 tablespoons plain yogurt
2 tablespoons honey
¼ teaspoon cinnamon

Serving: 1/4 Recipe	Calories: 109
Protein: 1 gm	Fat: 0.5 gm
Carbs: 28 gm	Cholesterol: 0 mg
Sodium: 20 mg	Calcium: 35 mg

1.  In a large mixing bowl, grate carrots and apple, and discard the core. Add raisins and lemon juice, stir.

2. In a separate mixing bowl, blend yogurt, honey and cinnamon. Stir into carrot-apple-raisin mixture. Chill well.

Take A Look

Did you know that a leaf's jagged edges help catch breezes? This cools the leaf and enhances its intake of carbon dioxide. Jagged edges also deter insects from munching on them.

DESSERTS & BEVERAGES

CHOCOLATE CHOCOLATE BROWNIES

Makes 18 Brownies

TOOLS:
measuring cups and spoons
small saucepan
2 medium mixing bowls
wooden spoon
8" x 8" non-stick pan
non-stick spray cooking oil

INGREDIENTS:
4 squares unsweetened
    Baker's chocolate
1 stick butter
1½ cups sugar
3 tablespoons water
1 egg
1 teaspoon vanilla extract
1⅓ cups all-purpose flour
¼ teaspoon salt
¼ teaspoon baking soda
¼ cup chocolate chips or
    chopped nuts

Serving: 1 Brownie	Calories: 200
Protein: 2 gm	Fat: 10 gm
Carbs: 28 gm	Cholesterol: 27 mg
Sodium: 112 mg	Calcium: 16 mg

Preheat oven to 350°.

1. In a small saucepan over medium-low heat, combine chocolate squares and butter. Stir frequently until everything has melted. Remove from heat.

2. In a bowl, beat sugar, water, egg and vanilla. Stir in melted mixture.

3. In a separate bowl, mix together flour, salt and baking soda.

4. Stir half of the flour mixture into the liquid mixture until blended, then stir in remaining flour mixture. Mix in chocolate chips or chopped nuts.

5. Spray pan with non-stick cooking oil. Pour batter into pan. Bake 25-30 minutes, or until a toothpick inserted in center of brownies comes out clean.

Take A Look

Create memorable family moments by sharing a sunrise, spending an evening under the stars, playing in a gentle rain, picking out cloud formations, or volunteering to clean up a park together.

Animal Fact

To domesticate an animal is to train or adapt it to live in a human environment so it can be of use to human beings. Camels were domesticated over 4,000 years ago. They have provided meat, milk, wool and hides to desert and mountain dwelling people ever since. Camels belong to the animal family Camelidae which includes the one-humped (dromedary) and the two-humped (Bactrian) camels. Camelidae also includes the llama and the vicuna, which is similar to the llama and lives in the Andes. The growth of civilization has greatly reduced the territory where wild camel herds live, but domesticated camels thrive in Africa, Asia, South America and Australia. To protect their eyes from sand blowing in the desert winds, camels have long eyelashes that catch most of the sand. They also have an extra eyelid that moves from side to side and wipes their eyes clean of sand. Camels are famous for their ability to survive without drinking water for long periods of time. You may have heard that camels store water in their humps, but that's not true. They are just really good at conserving water. Their humps are actually a place for storing fat, which is a source of energy for the camel.

GINGERBREAD PEOPLE

Makes 1 Dozen Gingerbread People

TOOLS:

large mixing bowl
electric mixer
measuring cups and spoons
rolling pin
cookie cutters
non-stick spray cooking oil
cookie sheet and spatula
wire cooling rack

INGREDIENTS:

½ cup sugar
¼ cup canola oil
½ cup dark molasses
¼ cup water
½ teaspoon salt
2 teaspoons ground ginger
½ teaspoon baking soda
½ teaspoon allspice
2½ cups all-purpose flour
raisins and small candies

1. In a large mixing bowl, beat sugar, oil, molasses and water on low speed with electric mixer until blended. Add salt, ginger, baking soda, allspice and flour, blend at medium speed 1 minute. Cover bowl and refrigerate 1 hour.

2. Preheat oven to 350°. Spray cookie sheet with non-stick cooking oil.

3. Lightly sprinkle table or countertop with flour. Roll out dough with a rolling pin until about ¼ inch thick.

4. Cut out shapes with cookie cutters. Carefully lift cookies with spatula onto cookie sheet.

5. Decorate Gingerbread People with raisins and candies. Bake on upper oven rack for 8-10 minutes.

6. Use oven mitts to remove the cookie sheet from oven. Let *Gingerbread People* cool on cookie sheet for 2 minutes. Carefully remove cookies with spatula to cool on wire rack.

When cookies have cooled to room temperature you can add frosting.

Nutritional Analysis does not include decorations
Serving: 1 Cookie   Calories: 198
Protein: 3 gm   Fat: 5 gm
Carbs: 36 gm   Cholesterol: 0 mg
Sodium: 24 mg   Calcium: 99 mg

Animal Fact

The red fox ranges from the Arctic to the southern United States. Unlike its fellow dogs, the red fox hunts alone, relying on its ability to quietly sneak up on prey, then suddenly leaping out like a cat. Preferring small rodents and rabbits, it also eats insects and berries when necessary. Baby fox are called kits. Both the female and male are excellent parents. The father fox is very attentive to his kits after they are weaned. Researchers report seeing dads being very excited about their young, playing with them endlessly. One father was even observed waiting for a watchful mother to fall asleep, then quietly calling to his kits to come play with him. It isn't all fun and games though. The fox father takes his responsibilities seriously, teaching his offspring survival skills. Their play often incorporates "games" that teach the kits to hunt and to escape danger. One such game could be called "hide and seek." The father fox hides food by burying it and the kits sniff and forage around until they find it.

DANDY CANDY CHEWS

Packed with energy and good for you, too!

Makes 1 Dozen Candies

TOOLS:
mixing bowl and wax paper
measuring cups and spoons
wooden spoon
small serving plate

INGREDIENTS:
2 tablespoons smooth
   peanut butter
¼ cup honey
½ cup granola (try *Cruncha Muncha Granola*, page 114)
¼ cup raisins
¼ cup coconut

Serving: 1 Candy	Calories: 77
Protein: 2 gm	Fat: 3 gm
Carbs: 12 gm	Cholesterol: 0 mg
Sodium: 15 mg	Calcium: 7 mg

1. In the mixing bowl, blend together peanut butter and honey with the wooden spoon.

2. Add granola and raisins, and stir until well mixed.

3. Cover with wax paper and chill in the refrigerator 30 minutes. (Chilling makes it easier to handle.)

4. When completely cold, take a spoonful of the candy mixture, give it a squeeze in your fist and roll it into a small ball between your palms. Roll ball in coconut. Place candy on serving plate. Make candy balls until all the mixture is used.

5. Cover plate and chill at least 1 hour.

Take a Dandy Candy Chew along in your lunchbox for a high-energy snack.

Food Fact

After collecting nectar from flowers, bees temporarily store it in their stomachs where enzymes transform the nectar into honey. The color and flavor of the honey are determined by the flowers from which the nectar is taken. For example, Orange Blossom honey comes from bees that are pollinating orange trees, and Wildflower honey from the nectar of many flowers. Have you tasted the sweetness of Apple Blossom, Blueberry or Tupelo Honey?

Helping Hands

Adopt a tree! Choose a tree in your yard or neighborhood.
- Photograph the tree each season.
- Collect or draw a picture of a fallen twig, a leaf, a bud in spring, and a fruit or seed in autumn.
- Take rubbings of the leaves and bark using a soft pencil and paper.
- Find out how old your tree is by measuring around the trunk at about 3 feet above the ground. Every inch equals about 1 year.
- Check out a field guide from your local library and identify what kinds of plants and animals live in and around your tree.
- Watch the wildlife that visits the tree. Nature observers are very quiet so they don't scare off what they're trying to observe.

NO-BAKE OATMEAL COOKIES

Makes 3 Dozen Cookies

TOOLS:
measuring cups and spoons
medium saucepan
wooden spoon
cookie sheet and wax paper

INGREDIENTS:
2 cups sugar
3 tablespoons cocoa powder
4 tablespoons butter
½ cup 2% lowfat milk
½ teaspoon vanilla extract
½ cup peanut butter
3 cups dry rolled quick oats

1. In medium saucepan, combine sugar, cocoa, butter and milk.

2. Stir constantly over medium-high heat until mixture comes to a rolling boil (be careful, it will be really bubbly). Boil 1 minute, then remove from heat.

3. Stir in vanilla and peanut butter until peanut butter is melted. Mix in oats.

4. Place a sheet of wax paper on cookie sheet and drop spoonfuls of *No-Bake Oatmeal Cookies* onto wax paper. Flatten slightly with the back of spoon. Chill 45 minutes.

*Substitute peppermint extract
for vanilla extract
for a chocolate-mint treat!*

Serving: 2 Cookies	Calories: 212
Protein: 4 gm	Fat: 7.5 gm
Carbs: 34 gm	Cholesterol: 8 mg
Sodium: 70 mg	Calcium: 14 mg

Take A Look

Storytelling is an important part of the world's cultures, and many stories are passed down from generation to generation. Folktales are stories that explain things not scientifically understood. An African folktale describes how God created the hippo and told it to cut down the grass for the other animals. When the hippo discovered how hot Africa was, it asked God if it could stay in the water during the day and cut grass at night. God agreed, and that's why the hippo feeds at night. Can you make up a folktale to explain the behavior of an animal?

Ecology Fact

Energy is vital for basic needs such as cooking, heating and transportation. Some energy-producing methods can seriously damage the environment. Safer and cleaner forms of energy production are being introduced in many countries, including the burning of industrial waste and consumer refuse. Other forms of energy production are renewable energy sources, meaning they will not run out as will the Earth's supply of fossil fuels. Renewable energy sources include solar energy, wind, wave and tidal energy. Energy conservation is something your family can do.

1) Don't waste electricity. Turn off lights when not in use. Take a shower instead of a bath, it uses less heated water.

2) Insulate hot water tanks and pipes. The water will heat up quicker and stay hot longer.

3) Insulate your attic, and draft-proof doors and windows. This saves up to 20% of your energy bill (leaving more money for fun things!)

NO-BAKE ZEBRA CAKE

This amazingly simple recipe is <u>so</u> yummy!

Serves 6

TOOLS:
cake platter with tall cover
rubber spatula

INGREDIENTS:
12 chocolate lowfat
   graham crackers (don't
   break them apart)
1 recipe *Quick & Easy*
   Frosting, page 91

Serving: 1/6 Recipe
Protein: 4 gm
Carbs: 28 gm
Sodium: 199 mg

Calories: 179
Fat: 5.5 gm
Cholesterol: 15 mg
Calcium: 46 mg

1. Frost 2 graham cracker rectangles. Place them next to each other with edges touching on the cake platter.

2. Place 2 more graham crackers side by side, turned to cross over the frosted ones. Frost the tops of these.

3. Repeat step 2, turning each layer, until all the graham crackers are used.

4. Once all graham crackers are stacked and frosted, frost the top and sides of your cake.

5. Cover platter and chill at least 6 hours or overnight. Slice cake into 6 pieces, serve with tall glasses of milk.

While chilling in the refrigerator the graham crackers absorb moisture from the frosting and become like cake.

Take A Look

Plants have unique ways of distributing their seeds. The dandelion has feathery seeds that fly away on the wind. Others have seed pods that explode when ripe, scattering their seeds a great distance. Seeds of edible fruits are distributed in the droppings of the birds and animals that eat them. Can you identify how plants in your yard distribute seeds?

QUICK & EASY FROSTING

Makes 1½ Cups Frosting

TOOLS:
measuring cups and spoons
small mixing bowl
fork

INGREDIENTS:
¾ cup lowfat cream cheese
1 cup powdered sugar
1 teaspoon vanilla extract
2 tablespoons 2% lowfat milk

Soften cream cheese by taking it out of the refrigerator about an hour before making frosting.

1. In a small mixing bowl, mash cream cheese with powdered sugar.

2. Add vanilla and milk. Mix until completely smooth.

It really is that quick & easy!

Serving: 4 Tablespoons   Calories: 153
Protein: 3 gm   Fat: 5 gm
Carbs: 22 gm   Cholesterol: 15 mg
Sodium: 153 mg   Calcium: 46 mg

Animal Fact

Zebras, wild asses and Mongolian wild horses are true wild horses. These animals live on the open grasslands and along the edges of deserts of eastern and southern Africa. When threatened, the zebra, like other wild horses, depends on its strong legs to run to safety. As the zebra runs it zigzags from side to side, looking back over its shoulder to see if it is still being chased. A zebra's stripes create an optical illusion, which may provide protective camouflage. The disruptive pattern also helps the zebra to "disappear" in haze or low light. Zebras are grazing animals, eating huge amounts of any available grasses. They spend the day eating and resting, and sleep at night is interspersed with periods of grazing.

PEAR-GINGERSNAP DELIGHT

This recipe is fast and party fancy!

Serves 4

TOOLS:
can opener
strainer
paper bag
rolling pin
small bowl
4 dessert dishes

INGREDIENTS:
4 canned pear halves
10 gingersnap cookies
½ cup whipped topping

Serving: 1 Dish	Calories: 139
Protein: 1 gm	Fat: 3.5 gm
Carbs: 25 gm	Cholesterol: 0 mg
Sodium: 124 mg	Calcium: 19 mg

1. Drain pears in strainer, and save the juice.

2. Put gingersnap cookies in a small paper bag. Fold down the top of the bag so bag is smooth and flat. Roll a rolling pin over the bag until the cookies are finely crushed.

3. Pour the cookie crumbs into a small bowl. Roll pear halves in the crumbs until they are covered completely.

4. Place each pear half in a dessert dish and top with whipped topping.

Your guests will be impressed!

Cooking Tip

When draining liquid from canned fruit, reserve (save) liquid to flavor fruit juice or popsicles. Reserve vegetable liquids to flavor soups and stews; fill ice cube trays with reserved vegetable liquid and freeze. Store frozen cubes in a plastic bag in the freezer. To use frozen vegetable juice cubes, just drop them in with other liquids to thaw.

🖐 Helping Hands 🖐

Trees are a valuable resource. How many things in your home come from trees? Be sure to notice the furniture, food boxes, notepads, matches, pencils... Although trees are a renewable resource, they are being harvested faster than new ones can be grown. Help preserve trees by:

1) Using both sides of paper when drawing or coloring.

2) Recycling newspaper into paper you can use for art or stationery! Turn to page 136 to learn how.

3) Reusing paper bags and packaging instead of throwing them away.

4) Taking good care of what you already have. When something is broken or worn out, repair it instead of buying new.

PEACH CRISP

Serves 9

TOOLS:

8" x 8" baking dish
non-stick spray cooking oil
cutting board and knife
large mixing bowl and spoon
measuring cups and spoons

INGREDIENTS:

8 peaches
3 tablespoons raisins
½ cup sugar
1 tablespoon lemon juice
¾ cup dry rolled oats
3 tablespoons chopped
    pecans
⅓ cup packed brown sugar
¼ teaspoon cinnamon
2 tablespoons all-purpose
    flour
2 tablespoons melted butter

Preheat oven to 375°.

1. Spray baking dish with non-stick cooking oil.

2. Ask an adult to peel, pit and slice the peaches into wedges.

3. Place peach wedges in the mixing bowl. Add raisins, sprinkle with sugar and lemon juice. Stir to coat peaches, then spread into the baking dish.

4. In the mixing bowl, combine oats, pecans, brown sugar, cinnamon and flour. Pour in melted butter and stir until mixture is crumbly.

5. Sprinkle crumb mixture over peaches. Bake 25-30 minutes.

6. Use oven mitts to remove from oven. Cool 10 minutes before serving.

Substitute apples for the peaches and "voilà," you have Apple Crisp!

Serving: 1/9 Recipe
Protein: 3 gm
Carbs: 41 gm
Sodium: 32 mg

Calories: 212
Fat: 5 gm
Cholesterol: 7 mg
Calcium: 22 mg

Ecology Fact

The average incandescent light bulb is wasteful. Only about 10 percent of the electricity it uses turns into light, 90 percent of the energy is lost as heat! Compact fluorescent bulbs are much more efficient. One 18-watt compact fluorescent bulb produces as much light as an incandescent 60-watt bulb, and lasts 10 times longer. A compact fluorescent bulb costs more to purchase, but over its lifetime it can save as much as $50 in electrical bills and frequent bulb replacement costs. By reducing energy consumption, compact fluorescent bulbs can also reduce the emissions from pollution-generating power plants. Encourage your parents to replace standard bulbs with compact fluorescent bulbs. They'll save money and help the environment.

GRAPE SORBET

Serves 6

TOOLS:

measuring cups and spoons
small saucepan and spoon
8" x 8" baking pan
6 dessert dishes
small ice cream scooper

INGREDIENTS:

¾ cup water
2 tablespoons sugar
12-ounce can frozen grape
   juice concentrate
1 cup applesauce
fresh mint leaves (optional)

Serving: 1/6 Recipe
Protein: 1 gm
Carbs: 37 gm
Sodium: 7 mg

Calories: 147
Fat: 0.5 gm
Cholesterol: 0 mg
Calcium: 16 mg

1. Combine water and sugar in a small saucepan. Stir over low heat until sugar is dissolved.

2. Remove from heat and stir in grape juice concentrate and applesauce.

3. Pour into baking pan and set in freezer. Stir every 20 minutes for 1½ hours. The sorbet can now be served or left to freeze.

4. Use a small ice cream scooper to shape into balls. Place in serving dishes garnished with mint leaves, if desired.

Take A Look

There is still much exploration to be done on the southern continental ice cap of Antarctica. Nearly all of Antarctica is covered by an ice sheet which is up to 3 miles thick! The ice sheet contains 90% of world's ice and 70% of the Earth's fresh water.

JELL-POPS

This is a wobbly pop!

Serves 8

TOOLS:
measuring cups and spoons
small saucepan
wooden spoon
popsicle molds

INGREDIENTS:
2 cups fruit juice
  (grape, apple and pear
  juices are favorites)
2 tablespoons lemon gelatin

Serving: 1 Jell-Pop	Calories: 31
Protein: 0 gm	Fat: 0 gm
Carbs: 7 gm	Cholesterol: 0 mg
Sodium: 7 mg	Calcium: 4 mg

1. In a small saucepan, combine fruit juice with gelatin.

2. Cook on medium-low heat, stirring constantly, until gelatin is completely dissolved.

3. Remove from heat and cool at room temperature for 5 minutes. Pour liquid into popsicle molds or small paper cups.

4. Freeze until set. (If using paper cups, freeze until just firm enough for popsicle sticks to stand up, then insert sticks.)

To remove pops from molds, warm with the palms of your hands or briefly dunk into a bowl of lukewarm water.

 ## Animal Fact

Penguins are high on the list of amusing animals, and it's easy to see why. Strutting around like funny little people in tuxedos, penguins remind us of ourselves at our silliest. Although they are covered in feathers, penguins cannot fly, but move quickly on ice by sliding on their stomachs. To keep moving they push with their wings and feet like a skier using ski poles. Some penguins live in the Antarctic Circle during the summer, then migrate to warmer locations for the winter. They may swim thousands of miles to get from place to place! Penguins depend on the oceans for their survival, for the fish they eat and as a safe haven from land predators. By caring for the Earth's oceans we help protect penguins.

JELLYFISH BOWLS

Serves 4

TOOLS:
measuring cups
medium mixing bowl
spoon
4 clear glasses or bowls
(to see the fish "swim")

INGREDIENTS:
1 package blue gelatin
24 gummy fish

Serving: 1/4 Recipe	Calories: 127
Protein: 3 gm	Fat: 0 gm
Carbs: 30 gm	Cholesterol: 0 mg
Sodium: 75 mg	Calcium: 1 mg

1. Make gelatin according to package directions. Place mixture in mixing bowl in refrigerator for 18 minutes.

2. Remove from refrigerator and gently stir in gummy fish.

3. Spoon into small clear glasses or bowls. Return to refrigerator until gelatin is set.

Animal Fact

Whales live in the ocean like fish, swim, hunt and even resemble fish. But, whales are NOT fish. Whales are mammals, just like people, but they are mammals that live in the sea. A mammal is an animal that has lungs and breathes air. Mammals are warmblooded, with a body temperature that is more or less the same all the time. The babies of mammals are born alive instead of being hatched from eggs (except the echidna and platypus). All mammal babies take milk from their mothers. The mother whale's milk is very rich, allowing her baby to gain as much as 10 pounds an hour!

CHOCOLATE PUDDING

Serves 4

TOOLS:
measuring cups and spoons
medium saucepan
whisk
4 dessert dishes

INGREDIENTS:
⅓ cup sugar
¼ cup cornstarch
¼ teaspoon salt
¼ cup cocoa powder
2 cans condensed nonfat
   milk
1 teaspoon vanilla extract
whipped topping

Serving: 1/4 Recipe   Calories: 205
Protein: 9 gm   Fat: 1.5 gm
Carbs: 38 gm   Cholesterol: 5 mg
Sodium: 289 mg   Calcium: 316 mg

1. Measure sugar, cornstarch, salt and cocoa powder into medium saucepan. Whisk in condensed milk, a little at a time, until completely blended and smooth.

2. Whisking constantly, bring the mixture to a boil over medium heat. Pudding burns if you stop stirring.

3. Reduce the heat to low. Gently simmer 2-3 minutes (keep stirring). Remove from heat.

4. Add vanilla. Cool pudding in saucepan for 5 minutes, stirring once or twice while waiting. Spoon ½ cup of pudding into each dessert dish. Chill to firm before serving. Serve with a dollop of whipped topping on each.

Food Fact

The seeds or "beans" of the tropical cacao tree are leathery pods that grow on its trunk and branches. Workers cut the pods from the tree with large knives called machetes. The purple or creamy white beans that are shelled from the pod have a raw bitter taste. After the beans are processed, cocoa butter is pressed from what is called the chocolate liquor, leaving behind a light brown cake of solid particles. This material is then ground and sifted to make cocoa powder.

OUTRAGEOUS ORANGE SHAKE

Serves 2

TOOLS:
measuring cups and spoons
blender
serving glasses

INGREDIENTS:
8 large scoops vanilla frozen
    yogurt or ice cream
1 cup 2% lowfat milk
4 tablespoons frozen
    orange juice concentrate
3 pinches cinnamon

Nutritional Analysis uses frozen yogurt
Serving: 1/2 Recipe	Calories: 292
Protein: 10 gm	Fat: 7 gm
Carbs: 49 gm	Cholesterol: 27 mg
Sodium: 115 mg	Calcium: 279 mg

1. Place 4 scoops frozen yogurt or ice cream into blender. Add milk, orange juice concentrate and cinnamon. Blend at medium speed until smooth.

2. Blend in remaining 4 scoops frozen yogurt or ice cream until creamy.

Serve in frosty tall glasses.

Take A Look

The tundra is a treeless area between the ice cap of the North Pole and the treeline of the arctic regions. The word "tundra" comes from a Finnish word meaning "barren land." For most of the year, temperatures on the tundra are below freezing. Winters are long and severe, and summer temperatures rarely exceed 50°. The underlying subsoil, called the permafrost, is always frozen. Only moss, lichen and some flowering plants grow in the brief summer sun. The caribou, snowshoe rabbit, arctic fox and polar bear are among the few animals able to survive in the extremely cold climate.

OTHER SHAKES

Make these substitutions for the orange juice concentrate and cinnamon.

Strawberry Shake:
½ cup mashed strawberries and 1 small banana.

Raspberry Shake:
⅓ cup mashed raspberries and 2 drops almond extract.

Peach Shake:
2 ripe peaches (peeled and pitted) and 2 tablespoons frozen pink lemonade concentrate.

Blueberry Shake:
⅓ cup blueberry pulp (from blueberries pressed through sieve to remove skins) and 2 pinches cinnamon.

LIMEADE SYRUP

TOOLS:
cutting board and knife
juicer
strainer
measuring cups
small saucepan
tall serving glasses

INGREDIENTS:
5 limes
¾ cup water
1 cup sugar

Serving: 1/4 Recipe	Calories: 210
Protein: 0 gm	Fat: 0 gm
Carbs: 56 gm	Cholesterol: 0 mg
Sodium: 3 mg	Calcium: 7 mg

Serves 4

1. Cut 4 of the limes in half. Squeeze the lime halves with the juicer. Pour juice through strainer to remove seeds.

2. Combine water and sugar in the saucepan. Boil 10 minutes, then cool to room temperature. Stir in lime juice. Chill 1-2 hours until syrupy.

3. Measure ¼ cup limeade syrup into each glass. Fill with ice water and stir.

4. Slice the last lime into ¼-inch-thick rounds. Cut rounds in half and hang one on the lip of each glass.

Replace limes with lemons for lemonade.

Food Fact

Years ago, seamen on long-distance voyages rarely had fresh fruits and vegetables to eat while at sea. These sailors often suffered from an illness which caused bruising, loss of hair and teeth, and painful muscles. Many sailors even died from the illness, which was called scurvy. A doctor in the British navy discovered that sailors who regularly drank citrus juice or ate oranges didn't get scurvy. The cure and prevention for this awful disease was vitamin C! British naval law was amended to require that a daily allowance of lime or lemon juice be given to sailors to prevent scurvy. This is why British sailors are called "limeys."

Animal Fact

You don't have to kiss a frog to consider it your prince. The "royal" appetite of frogs, toads and other amphibians is a welcome addition to any yard. Frogs devour a remarkable number of destructive insects and pests. Inviting frogs into your yard can greatly reduce insect pests without the use of pesticides. (Pesticides can be harmful to pets and children.) To attract frogs, provide an area with water and shade to get out of the sun. Creating a small garden pond with ferns growing alongside provides an ideal area for frogs to forage and hide. You can also turn an old terra-cotta pot upside down, and break out a "doorway." A pile of rocks arranged with a cavity inside makes an elegant "Toad Abode." Just remember to place these structures out of the sun and provide water each day.

PEACH FROSTY

Delicious and refreshing any time of year!

Serves 4

TOOLS:
knife and blender
measuring cups and spoons

INGREDIENTS:
3 ripe peaches or
   6 canned peach halves
½ cup frozen pink
   lemonade concentrate
10-12 ice cubes

Serving: 1/4 Recipe   Calories: 79
Protein: 0.5 gm   Fat: 0 gm
Carbs: 21 gm   Cholesterol: 0 mg
Sodium: 2 mg   Calcium: 5 mg

1. If using fresh peaches, ask an adult to peel, halve and pit them. For canned peaches, drain liquid.

2. Combine peaches, lemonade concentrate and 5-6 ice cubes in blender. Blend at medium speed until smooth, about 1 minute. (It may help to use the pulse button until the ice gets chopped up a bit.)

3. Add remaining ice and blend at high speed 45 seconds or until smooth. Pour into glasses and serve with a straw.

Cooking Tip
The peach's skin contains most of the fruit's nutrients and a lot of fiber. When the recipe allows, save vitamins, minerals, time and flavor - don't peel the peaches! If the recipe requires peeled peaches, here's an easy way to do it. With adult help, place the peaches in a large bowl and cover them with boiling water. Soak for 1 minute, then pour off the water. Make a cut around the circumference of the peach and the skin will slip off!

MARVELOUS MIXES

COOKIES, COOKIES, COOKIES

Makes 3 Dozen Cookies

TOOLS:

measuring cups and spoons
large mixing bowl
large mixing spoon
pastry blender
    or two butter knives

INGREDIENTS:

1½ cups all-purpose flour
1 teaspoon baking soda
½ teaspoon salt
¾ cup sugar
1 stick butter

Nutritional Analysis for *Sugar Cookies*
Serving: 2 Cookies   Calories: 123
Protein: 1 gm   Fat: 6 gm
Carbs: 16 gm   Cholesterol: 26 mg
Sodium: 194 mg   Calcium: 5 mg

1. Combine all ingredients, except butter, in the large mixing bowl. Stir with large mixing spoon.

2. Cut in butter with the pastry blender, or use two table knives by crossing blades and pulling past each other to distribute butter.

Cooking Tip

When doubling a recipe, increase spices by 50%. Taste, then add spices to taste. (Do not taste if mixture contains raw egg!)

106

ALL COOKIES: Bake at 375° on a non-stick cookie sheet 8-10 minutes.

Sugar Cookies:

Combine 1 recipe of *Cookies, Cookies, Cookies* mix with 1 egg, 1 tablespoon water and 1 teaspoon vanilla. Make 1-inch balls, roll in a bowl of sugar and place on cookie sheet. Gently flatten with floured bottom of a glass. Bake.

Cookie-Cutter Cookies:

Prepare dough for *Sugar Cookies* as shown above, then mix in ½ cup flour. On a lightly floured counter, roll dough ¼ inch thick with rolling pin. Cut with cookie cutters, sprinkle with sugar. Place on cookie sheet. Bake.

Peanut Butter Cookies:

Mix together 1 cup peanut butter, ½ cup brown sugar, 1 tablespoon water, 1 egg and 1 teaspoon vanilla. Combine with 1 prepared recipe of *Cookies, Cookies, Cookies* mix, add ½ cup flour and stir well. Roll into 1-inch balls, place on a cookie sheet. Press gently with a fork to slightly flatten. Bake.

Chocolate Chip Cookies:

Mix together ¾ cup packed light brown sugar, 1 egg, 2 tablespoons water and 1 teaspoon vanilla. Combine with 1 prepared recipe of *Cookies, Cookies, Cookies* mix. Blend well, then add 1½ cups semi-sweet chocolate chips and ½ cup chopped walnuts. Drop by the teaspoon onto cookie sheet. Bake.

Take A Look

The Alps are a mountain system in the heart of the European continent. These mountains curve in a huge arc though France, Italy, Switzerland, Germany and Austria. The Alps are known for their towering snow-capped peaks, pristine lakes and mountain meadows. The mountain range is home to over 3,500 species of plant life and many animal species. As the surrounding areas have become more industrialized, the levels of air pollution in the Alps have increased. Several European governments are promoting legislation to control these emissions and clean the mountain air.

CRAZY CAKE

Makes Double-Layer Round Cake, or
9" x 13" Single-Layer Cake, or
24 Cupcakes

TOOLS:
measuring cups and spoons
2 mixing bowls
electric mixer
rubber spatula

INGREDIENTS:
1 stick butter, softened
½ cup applesauce
2½ cups sugar
3½ cups all-purpose flour
1½ tablespoons baking
    powder
1 teaspoon baking soda
1 teaspoon salt
1 large egg
2 egg whites
½ cup buttermilk
1½ teaspoons vanilla extract

1. Combine butter, applesauce and sugar in a mixing bowl. Use the electric mixer at medium speed to beat for 1 minute. Blend until smooth. (This is called creaming.)

2. Measure the flour into another bowl. Use spatula to mix in baking powder, baking soda and salt.

3. Add a small amount of the flour mixture to the creamed mixture and beat at medium speed until thoroughly mixed. Repeat this step until all the flour mixture has been blended in. Occasionally scrape down the sides of the bowl.

4. On medium speed, beat in egg, egg whites, buttermilk and vanilla.

Nutritional Analysis for *White Cake*
(does not include cake frosting)

Serving: 1/12 Recipe	Calories: 383
Protein: 5 gm	Fat: 9 gm
Carbs: 71 gm	Cholesterol: 39 mg
Sodium: 550 mg	Calcium: 75 mg

Cooking Tip
Insert a toothpick into the center of the cake when you think it is done. If it is, the toothpick will come out clean and not gooey.

White Cake: Prepare *Crazy Cake* recipe. Follow baking directions below.

Lemon Cake: Prepare *Crazy Cake* recipe, and add 1 tablespoon lemon juice and 2 tablespoons sugar to batter. Follow baking directions below.

Chocolate Cake: Prepare *Crazy Cake* recipe, and add 2 tablespoons milk and 3 tablespoons cocoa powder to batter. Follow baking directions below.

Spice Cake: Prepare *Crazy Cake* recipe, and add ½ teaspoon cinnamon, ½ teaspoon ground cloves and ¼ teaspoon nutmeg to batter. Follow baking directions below.

BAKING DIRECTIONS FOR ALL CAKES:

Select non-stick cake pans: Two 8" or 9" round pans, or one 9" x 13" pan. For 24 cupcakes: Select muffin tins and fill with paper cupcake liners.

Preheat oven to 350°.

Spread batter evenly in pans or spoon into cupcake liners.

Bake: 8" or 9" round cakes or cupcakes for 20-25 minutes.
      9" x 13" cake for 25-30 minutes.

Cool in pan for 10 minutes before flipping onto wire cooling racks. Cool completely before frosting.

To Frost Single-Layer Cake and Cupcakes: Use *Quick & Easy Frosting*, page 91, or purchase prepared frosting. Spread evenly using a small spatula.

To Frost Double-Layer Round Cake: Place one cake upside-down on cake platter. Frost top side of this cake. Place second cake right side up on top of the frosted cake. Frost top and sides of your Double-Layer Cake!

BASIC BISCUITS & MORE

TOOLS:
mixing bowl and pastry cutter
measuring cups and spoons
non-stick baking sheet

INGREDIENTS:
2¼ cups all-purpose flour
½ cup dry powdered milk
1 tablespoon baking powder
1 tablespoon sugar
4 tablespoons butter
½ cup buttermilk

Nutritional Analysis for *Cut Biscuits*
Serving: 1 Biscuit   Calories: 138
Protein: 4 gm   Fat: 4.5 gm
Carbs: 21 gm   Cholesterol: 11 mg
Sodium: 60 mg   Calcium: 43 mg

Combine flour, powdered milk, baking powder and sugar in mixing bowl. Cut in butter until evenly mixed. Use a fork to blend in buttermilk, forming a soft dough.

Cut Biscuits: Makes 12 Biscuits
Preheat oven to 350°.

1. On a lightly floured surface, knead dough 4 or 5 times. Roll or pat out the dough to be about ½ inch thick.

2. Cut with a biscuit cutter or twist out round biscuit shapes with inverted floured drinking glass. Bake on a non-stick cookie sheet for 10-12 minutes.

Drop Biscuits:
Makes 12 Biscuits

Prepare 1 recipe *Basic Biscuits & More*, then add ¼ cup more buttermilk. Drop spoonfuls of dough onto non-stick baking sheet. Bake 10-12 minutes at 350°.

Cinnamon Rolls:
Makes 12 Rolls

Prepare 1 recipe *Basic Biscuits & More*. Use a rolling pin to roll out dough on a lightly floured counter into a 9" x 9" x ¼"-thick-square. Spread a thin layer of butter over rolled dough. Sprinkle generously with brown sugar, cinnamon and raisins. Roll up like a log. Cut into twelve ¾-inch-thick rounds. Place on cookie sheet and bake at 350° for 10-12 minutes.

Pancakes:
Makes 12 Pancakes

Prepare 1 recipe *Basic Biscuits & More*, then add 1 egg, 3 tablespoons honey, 1 egg white and 1 cup milk or buttermilk. Blend with a fork. Cook pancakes according to instructions on page 10, beginning with step 3.

Muffins:
Makes 12 Muffins

Prepare 1 recipe *Basic Biscuits & More*, then add ⅓ cup honey, 1¾ cups milk and 1 egg. Blend with a fork. To *JAZZ* up your muffins, add your choice of ½ cup raisins, drained crushed pineapple, grated carrots, chopped dates, or blueberries dusted in 1 tablespoon flour. Spoon into non-stick muffin tins. Bake at 375° for 18-20 minutes.

Take A Look

A few lakes, like the Great Salt Lake and the Dead Sea, are more salty than the oceans. Most lakes contain fresh water and were formed by glaciers, volcanos or man. Lakes provide great outdoor recreation on hot summer days. One freshwater lake is Moosehead, the largest lake in Maine. It is a freshwater lake formed by glacial activity and named Moosehead because its shape is similar to Moose antlers.

BREAD

Makes 2 Loaves

TOOLS:
measuring cups and spoons
small and large mixing bowls
non-stick spray cooking oil
plastic wrap
2 bread pans (5" x 9")
wire cooling racks

INGREDIENTS:
2 cups very warm water
  (see cooking tip at right)
1 tablespoon sugar or honey
1 tablespoon active dry yeast
6½-7 cups all-purpose flour
1 tablespoon salt

1. Pour 2 cups very warm water into small bowl. Add sugar or honey, and stir to dissolve. Stir in yeast, then set aside for 5-6 minutes to activate yeast. The yeast will be frothy on top of the water when it is activated.

2. Measure 5½ cups flour into the large mixing bowl. Mix in the salt.

3. Stir yeast mixture into the flour. The dough will clump into a ball.

4. Place the dough ball on a lightly floured surface. Knead for 3-4 minutes, adding flour when dough becomes sticky. Stop kneading for a few minutes to let the dough rest. Spray two bread pans with non-stick cooking oil.

5. Knead dough another 3-4 minutes, adding a little more flour. Divide dough in half. Roll into loaf shapes and place in bread pans. Spray tops with non-stick cooking oil and loosely cover with plastic wrap. Allow bread to rise in a warm location for 45 minutes (on top of the refrigerator or dryer are warm locations). Bread is done rising when it has doubled in bulk. You can also test it by gently poking your finger into the dough. If it doesn't spring back, it has completed the rising process.

6. Preheat oven to 350°. Bake loaves for 40 minutes. Remove from oven and cool 10 minutes in pans, then tip out breads onto wire cooling racks.

1 Loaf Bread = 12 Slices
Serving: 1 Slice
Protein: 4 gm
Carbs: 26 gm
Sodium: 292 mg

Calories: 125
Fat: 0.5 gm
Cholesterol: 0 mg
Calcium: 6 mg

For a soft crust, brush tops with melted butter after removing loaves from the oven.

112

Cooking Tip

Two tips for successful bread making:

1) Don't kill the yeast, it is a sensitive fungus. If the water is too hot, the yeast will be killed. If the water is too cold, the yeast won't activate. Very warm (not scalding) tap water of 100°-110° is ideal.

2) Use the right amount of flour. Too much flour and the bread will be heavy and dry. Too little flour and it won't have enough body to hold itself up. Bread making is an art learned over time; keep practicing!

Pizza Dough:

1. Follow directions for bread through step 3, then add 2 tablespoons olive oil. Let dough rise in covered mixing bowl 45 minutes.

2. Knead dough 3-4 minutes, then divide in half. Use your fingers to spread each half on a pizza pan or a cookie sheet.

3. Cover dough with pizza sauce, grated cheese and veggies. Bake at 475° for 10-12 minutes.

Breadsticks:

1. Prepare step 1 of Pizza Dough.

2. Use a rolling pin to roll dough on a lightly floured counter into a ½-inch-thick square. Brush with olive oil, and sprinkle with grated Mozzarella or Parmesan cheese.

3. Use a pizza cutter to cut into 1½-inch-wide strips. Place strips on non-stick baking sheet. Let rise 30 minutes in a warm place. Bake at 350° for about 12 minutes.

CRUNCHA MUNCHA GRANOLA

Makes 5 Cups Granola

TOOLS:

measuring cups and spoons
large mixing bowl and spoon
2 non-stick cookie sheets
spatula

INGREDIENTS:

3 cups dry rolled oats
½ cup all-purpose flour
½ cup all-bran cereal,
    wheat germ or bran
½ cup raisins
¼ cup chopped dates or
    flaked coconut
¼ cup chopped walnuts
1 teaspoon cinnamon
½ cup maple syrup
¼ cup canola oil
¼ cup defrosted apple
    juice concentrate
2 teaspoons vanilla

Preheat oven to 325°.

1. In the mixing bowl, combine oats, flour, cereal or bran, raisins, dates or coconut, walnuts and cinnamon. Drizzle liquid ingredients over mixture. Stir until mixed well.

2. Spread half of the mixture evenly on each cookie sheet. Bake 10 minutes. Use oven mitts to remove cookie sheets from oven. Stir granola with the spatula.

3. Return cookie sheets to oven and bake 8 minutes more. Watch carefully to be sure granola does not burn.

4. When granola is finished baking, use oven mitts to remove from oven and stir with spatula. Cool on cookie sheets 15 minutes before eating or storing.

5. Store granola up to 3 months in an airtight container.

Serve with milk for a morning cereal, or stir Cruncha Muncha Granola into vanilla yogurt.

Serving: 1/2 Cup
Protein: 6 gm
Carbs: 47 gm
Sodium: 34 mg

Calories: 282
Fat: 9 gm
Cholesterol: 0 mg
Calcium: 51 mg

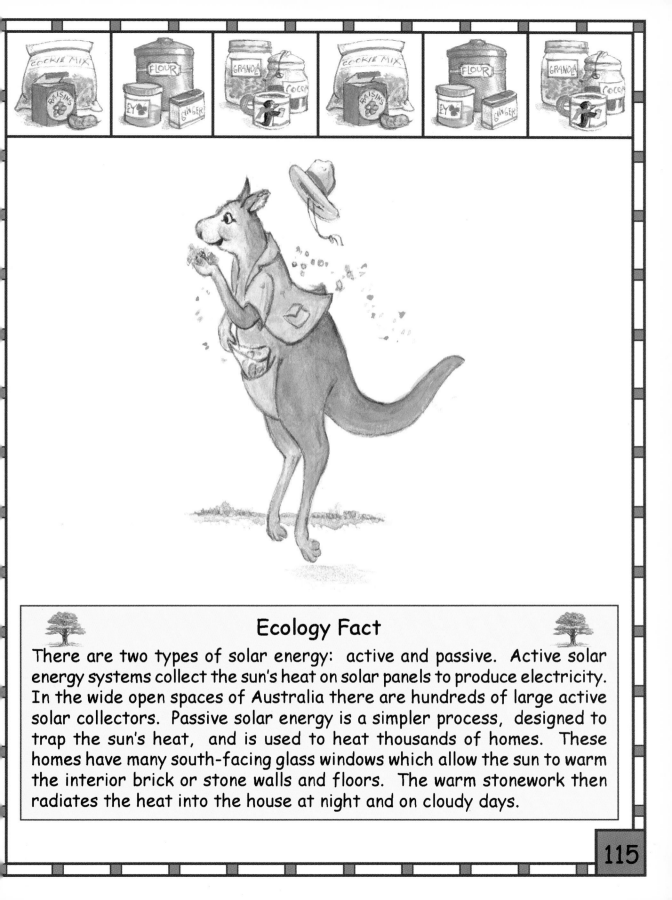

Ecology Fact

There are two types of solar energy: active and passive. Active solar energy systems collect the sun's heat on solar panels to produce electricity. In the wide open spaces of Australia there are hundreds of large active solar collectors. Passive solar energy is a simpler process, designed to trap the sun's heat, and is used to heat thousands of homes. These homes have many south-facing glass windows which allow the sun to warm the interior brick or stone walls and floors. The warm stonework then radiates the heat into the house at night and on cloudy days.

HOT COCOA MIX

Makes 15 Prepared Cups

TOOLS:
measuring cups and spoons

INGREDIENTS:
⅔ cup sugar

⅔ cup unsweetened cocoa
 powder

3 cups powdered skim milk

½ teaspoon salt

Nutritional Analysis for prepared Hot Cocoa
Serving: 1 Cup   Calories: 107
Protein: 3 gm   Fat: 2.5 gm
Carbs: 18 gm   Cholesterol: 1 mg
Sodium: 121 mg   Calcium: 74 mg

1. Thoroughly mix all ingredients. Store in an airtight container.

2. To make Hot Cocoa, measure ¼ cup *Hot Cocoa Mix* into a mug filled with 1 cup boiling water. Stir to dissolve.

Top with marshmallow fluff or mini-marshmallows.

HOT COCOA VARIATIONS:

Prepare a cup of Hot Cocoa, and stir into it any of the following:

Mexican Hot Chocolate:
Stir hot chocolate with a long cinnamon stick.

Hazelnut Hot Chocolate:
⅛ teaspoon hazelnut extract and a drop of vanilla extract.

Almond Hot Chocolate:
⅛ teaspoon almond extract.

Orange Hot Chocolate:
¼ teaspoon finely grated orange peel and a pinch of cinnamon.

Mint Hot Chocolate:
Stir hot chocolate with a peppermint stick or candy cane.

Ecology Fact

The Earth's climate is changing, causing concern among some scientists and conservationists. Wealthier nations depend on fossil fuels (gasoline and oil) to provide energy. The burning of fossil fuels has greatly increased the amount of carbon dioxide in the atmosphere. With the destruction of the rain forests, there are also fewer trees to utilize the excess carbon dioxide. This excess carbon dioxide in the atmosphere is trapping the sun's heat and warming the Earth. This process is called global warming. Some experts predict that a warmer ocean may melt the polar ice caps and raise sea levels, causing flooding in coastal areas. Other effects may be major changes in climate and agricultural growing cycles. Help slow the process of global warming by using less fuel.

CHILI SEASONING MIX

Makes 1 Cup (4 Batches) Chili Seasoning Mix

TOOLS:
measuring cups and spoons
airtight container

INGREDIENTS:
¾ cup all-purpose flour
½ cup dried minced onion
2 tablespoons chili powder
2 teaspoons curry powder
2 teaspoons garlic powder
2 teaspoons sugar
2 teaspoons red pepper
   flakes

Nutritional Analysis for prepared Filling
Serving: 1/4 Recipe   Calories: 174
Protein: 8 gm   Fat: 1.5 gm
Carbs: 33 gm   Cholesterol: 8 mg
Sodium: 451 mg   Calcium: 85 mg

Combine all ingredients in an airtight container. Shake well to mix.

To Make Taco or Burrito Filling:

1. In a saucepan over medium heat, warm 1 tablespoon canola oil. Sauté ½ cup chopped onion and ½ cup chopped green pepper for 5 minutes.

2. In a small cup, blend ¼ cup *Chili Seasoning Mix* with ½ cup warm water. Add mixture to saucepan.

3. Mix in 16-oz. can crushed tomatoes and 2 cups canned refried beans. Stir constantly until filling is hot.

Stuff tacos or roll burritos with filling. Serve with shredded lettuce, chopped tomatoes, salsa and grated cheese.

To Make ¼ Cup (1 Batch) Chili Seasoning Mix:

3 tablespoons all-purpose flour
2 tablespoons dried minced onion
1½ teaspoons chili powder
½ teaspoon curry powder
½ teaspoon garlic powder
½ teaspoon sugar
½ teaspoon red pepper flakes

SPAGHETTI SAUCE SEASONING

Makes 1 Cup (4 Batches) Sauce Seasoning

TOOLS:
measuring spoons
airtight container

INGREDIENTS:
4 tablespoons minced dried onion
2 teaspoons salt
2 teaspoons pepper
4 teaspoons garlic powder
4 tablespoons dried parsley
3 tablespoons dried basil
4 teaspoons dried oregano

Nutritional Analysis for prepared Sauce
Serving: 1/4 Recipe   Calories: 51
Protein: 2 gm   Fat: 0 gm
Carbs: 10 gm   Cholesterol: 0 mg
Sodium: 595 mg   Calcium: 84 mg

Combine all ingredients in an airtight container. Shake to mix well.

To Make Spaghetti Sauce:

To each 2 cups of crushed tomatoes, add ¼ cup *Spaghetti Sauce Seasoning*. Simmer 30 minutes. Serve over pasta.

For ¼ Cup (1 Batch) Spaghetti Sauce Seasoning:

1 tablespoon minced dried onion
½ teaspoon salt
½ teaspoon pepper
1 teaspoon garlic powder
1 tablespoon dried parsley
¾ tablespoon dried basil
1 teaspoon dried oregano

Take A Look

You don't need to go on a safari to see a lot of wildlife. Cities have been developed on land that once was exclusively animal habitat. Many animals have adapted to live in the cities with people. Some live in parks and others in open areas. Other animals live in or around buildings. Many birds build their nests beneath the roof eaves, on top of buildings, and even under bridge overpasses. City animals are often safer from predators who don't dare to enter the city. Take a look around your city or town. What kinds of wildlife are living there?

119

SHAKE-IT-UP BREADING MIX

Makes Breading for 2 Cups Veggies or 1 Pound Chicken or Fish Fillets

TOOLS:

measuring cups and spoons
small paper bag

INGREDIENTS:

1 cup breadcrumbs
¼ cup Parmesan cheese
¼ teaspoon black pepper

Nutritional Analysis for Onion Rings
Serving: 1/4 Recipe   Calories: 178
Protein: 9 gm   Fat: 4.5 gm
Carbs: 26 gm   Cholesterol: 59 mg
Sodium: 312 mg   Calcium: 132 mg

Combine ingredients in a small paper bag. Shake well to mix.

To Make Breaded Veggies, Chicken or Fish:

1. Add complementary seasonings to the bag of breading mix. For example, add ¼ teaspoon grated lemon rind for fish, parsley flakes for chicken, or garlic powder to add zip to vegetables. Be creative, try new combinations!

2. Prepare veggies, chicken or fish fillets by cutting into 1-inch chunks. (To Make Onion Rings: Peel 2 large onions. Slice into ¼-inch-thick rounds. Pop apart to separate rings.)

3. In a bowl, make a coating by beating together 1 egg, 1 egg white and 2 tablespoons milk. Dip cut items into coating, then place in the breading bag. Hold bag closed and shake to coat.

4. Bake 10 minutes on non-stick cookie sheet at 400°. Use oven mitts to remove from oven. Turn breaded items to bake 5 minutes on the other side.

To Prepare Breadcrumbs:

Preheat oven to 275°.

1. Place 4 slices of bread on a cookie sheet. Bake for 20 minutes or until bread is dry and crispy.

2. Use oven mitts to remove from oven and cool completely. Break bread into chunks and place them between layers of wax paper. Roll with a rolling pin until crushed to the consistency you desire.

*Crushed cornflakes can be substituted or added to breadcrumbs.
They make an extra-crispy coating too!*

Animal Fact

The three main species of seals are true seals, sea lions and fur seals. While there are many similarities among the species, certain characteristics differentiate them. Both the sea lion and fur seal have tiny earlobes, while true seals have none. On land, true seals pull themselves along with their front flippers or hunch their bodies and move like inchworms. Sea lions and fur seals can use both pairs of flippers (front and rear) to walk on land. All seals are mammals and breathe air. When swimming under the ice to look for food, they can hold their breath for almost an hour! Although once threatened, seal numbers are increasing for three reasons. Years ago, hunters killed so many seals that there were not enough animals left to justify the expense of hunting. Around the same time, electric lights were invented and the market for seal oil diminished. (Seal oil had been burned to provide light.) And fortunately, governments around the world made laws protecting the adorable seals.

BASIC DRESSING
The dressing possibilities are endless!

Makes 2 Cups

TOOLS:
measuring cups and spoons
1-quart jug or jar and lid

INGREDIENTS:
1½ teaspoons salt
1½ tablespoons sugar
½ teaspoon dry mustard
¼ cup vinegar
1 cup canola oil
¼ teaspoon onion powder
¼ teaspoon pepper

Measure all ingredients into jug or jar. Shake well to mix. Combine with additional ingredients on page 123 to make your selected dressing.

Each time you use the salad dressing be sure to shake it up (the oil and vinegar separate quickly).

Nutritional Analysis for French Dressing
Serving: 2 Tablespoons	Calories: 127
Protein: 1 gm	Fat: 9.5 gm
Carbs: 11 gm	Cholesterol: 0 mg
Sodium: 383 mg	Calcium: 9 mg

Animal Fact
Many butterflies and moths have spots on their wings. Some caterpillars have spots, too. The shape of the spots often resembles the eyes of a snake, and may serve to scare away owls and other predatory birds.

DRESSING VARIATIONS

French Dressing:
Combine 1¼ cups canned condensed tomato soup, ¼ cup sugar and 1 recipe of *Basic Dressing* in a jar. Shake well to mix. Chill before serving.

Parmesan Dressing:
Add ½ cup buttermilk, ½ cup sour cream, ½ cup finely grated Parmesan cheese to 1 recipe of *Basic Dressing*. Process in blender. Chill well.

Curry-Mustard Dressing:
Combine 1 cup sour cream, 1½ teaspoons curry, ½ teaspoon dry mustard and 1 recipe of *Basic Dressing* in a jar. Blend well. Chill before serving.

Spinach & Feta Cheese Dressing:
Add 6 tablespoons finely chopped fresh spinach, ¼ cup crumbled feta cheese to 1 recipe of *Basic Dressing*. Process in blender. Chill well.

Honey-Orange Dressing:
Combine 3 tablespoons honey, 2 tablespoons defrosted orange juice concentrate, 1 teaspoon grated orange peel and 1 recipe of *Basic Dressing* in a jar. Shake well to mix. Chill before serving.

Lemon-Poppy Seed Dressing:
Add 2 tablespoons lemon juice, 1 teaspoon grated lemon peel, 2 tablespoons poppy seeds, 2 tablespoons honey to 1 recipe of *Basic Dressing*. Process in blender. Chill before serving.

Oil-based dressings should be used sparingly, a little will go a long way.

SOUP SEASONING MIX

Makes Seasoning Mix For 4 Quarts of Soup

TOOLS:
measuring cups and spoons
airtight container

INGREDIENTS:
½ cup powdered vegetable
    bouillon
½ cup dried minced onion
1 tablespoon garlic powder
1 tablespoon thyme
1 tablespoon oregano
1 tablespoon ground sage
1 tablespoon rosemary
1 tablespoon marjoram
1 tablespoon ground basil
1 teaspoon black pepper

Nutritional Analysis for prepared Soup
Serving: 1/4 Soup Recipe Calories: 181
Protein: 3 gm   Fat: 0.5 gm
Carbs: 32 gm   Cholesterol: 0 mg
Sodium: 72 mg   Calcium: 172 mg

Combine all ingredients in an airtight container. Shake well. Use ½ cup *Soup Seasoning Mix* to season 1 quart (4 cups) soup. Store *Soup Seasoning Mix* in a dry place.

To Make 4 Servings of Soup:

1. In a large pot, add ½ cup *Soup Seasoning Mix* to 4 cups of chicken or vegetable broth.

2. Simmer broth over medium-high heat. Add 3 cups of finely chopped vegetables such as carrots, onion, broccoli, potatoes, turnip, celery, zucchini and cauliflower.

3. Simmer over medium-low heat until vegetables are cooked, about 20-30 minutes.

KITCHEN CRAFTS
& EXPERIMENTS

SUPER SOAP BUBBLES

TOOLS:
measuring cups and spoons
bucket

INGREDIENTS:
½ gallon water
½ cup Joy or Dawn
   dishwashing soap (other
   brands don't work as well)
1 teaspoon vegetable oil

Mix water, soap and vegetable oil in the bucket by gently swishing it around with your hand.

Now you're ready for some serious bubble blowing! Cool wet weather is best, early evenings and mornings are ideal. See the next page for some bubbly suggestions.

(Bubbles are great for "throwing" at the bride and groom instead of rice, and safer for people and birds, too.)

BUBBLE-BLOWING EQUIPMENT

Giant Bubbles:

Pour 3-4 cups of *Super Soap Bubbles* solution into a frying pan. (Don't use a non-stick pan or the finish will be ruined!) Bend a metal coat hanger into a loop that fits in the pan. Now dip the coat hanger loop into the solution and wave it in the air!

Square? Bubbles:

No, they don't really stay square but they do start out on a square frame. Thread a 2½-foot length of string through 2 straws, then tie ends of the string together. Hold the 2 straws together and dip into the *Super Soap Bubbles* solution. When you take them out, gently pull the straws apart and wave the straw through the air. Tip it up slightly to break off the bubbles.

Miniature Bubbles:

Trim the lip or edges off a 4"-6" plastic lid. Use a paper hole punch to punch holes in the lid. Dip lid into the *Super Soap Bubbles* solution and wave through the air. These tiny bubbles are magical!

Bubble Prints:

Pour 1 cup of *Super Soap Bubbles* solution into a small bowl. Set bowl on a large plate to catch the overflow of bubbles. Stir in a few drops of food coloring. Insert one end of a drinking straw into solution and blow. Bubbles will froth up over the top of the bowl. Lightly press white paper onto the bubbles. The bubbles will imprint the paper with the food coloring in bubble patterns. Lay the paper on flattened brown paper bags to dry. Use as gift wrap or stationery.

PLAY DOUGH

Don't make Play Dough or use paint on fine furniture!

TOOLS:
measuring cups and spoons
medium bowl
rolling pin
cookie cutters

INGREDIENTS:
⅓ cup salt
1⅓ cups flour
4 teaspoons liquid
  tempera paint
⅓ cup water
4 teaspoons dishwashing
  soap

1. In a medium bowl, mix together salt and flour until blended.

2. Add paint, water and soap to the flour mixture. Squeeze with your hands until everything is combined. Add a few drops of water if it seems too dry.

3. Use a rolling pin to roll out dough or pat it flat. Cut play dough with cookie cutters, or shape and sculpt your own original creations!

Make several batches of Play Dough in different colors. Store dough in an airtight container in the refrigerator.

PLAY CLAY

Do not make Play Clay on fine furniture surfaces!

TOOLS:
measuring cups
medium saucepan
wooden spoon
plate and a damp cloth

INGREDIENTS:
2 cups baking soda
1 cup cornstarch
1¼ cups cold water
4-5 drops food coloring

Take A Look

One of nature's most spectacular sculptures is the Grand Canyon in northwestern Arizona. Carved into solid rock by the Colorado River over millions of years, the canyon ranges from 4 to 18 miles wide. It is 217 miles long and up to a mile deep! Different kinds of rock make up the layers of the canyon walls. Each rock layer changes color throughout the day as the angle of the sun changes. Build up different colored layers of Play Clay or Play Dough. Carve it into jewelry, silly creatures, or a mini-Grand Canyon replica!

1. Combine all ingredients in a medium saucepan. Stir until well blended.

2. Cook over medium heat, stirring constantly, for 10-15 minutes or until mixture is the consistency of mashed potatoes. (If clay is over cooked, it may crack after drying.)

3. Remove pan from stove and spoon the clay mixture onto a plate. Cover plate with a damp cloth until clay is cool enough to handle.

4. Shape clay however you like. Roll it flat and cut out shapes, or mold it into 3-D ornaments and figures. To join pieces, dampen and scratch surfaces, then press together.

5. Dry molded *Play Clay* items overnight on a wire rack. To dry quickly, place items on a cookie sheet and bake in a 250° oven 10-15 minutes.

6. Paint *Play Clay* creations with poster or acrylic paint. Protect with a coat of clear acrylic or nail polish.

Unused Play Clay can be stored in an airtight container for up to 1 week.

129

FACE PAINT

TOOLS:
measuring spoons
muffin tin
6 popsicle sticks
small paint brushes

INGREDIENTS
FOR 6 COLORS:
2 tablespoons cornstarch
3 teaspoons water
1 tablespoon facial cold
   cream
6 different food colorings

1. Measure 1 teaspoon of cornstarch, ½ teaspoon water, ½ teaspoon cold cream and a few drops of one color food coloring into one of six muffin cups. Repeat process for each color. Stir each cup with a different popsicle stick until well mixed.

2. Now find a "canvas," maybe your brother or sister!

This Face Paint washes off nicely with a warm washcloth. The food coloring may leave a slight stain, but it will wear off in a day or two.

FINGER PAINT

TOOLS:
medium saucepan
measuring cups and spoons
spoon
small jars and lids
 (baby-food jars are ideal)

INGREDIENTS:
¾ cup cornstarch
3 cups cold water
1 tablespoon glycerine
 (available at pharmacies)
liquid tempera paints

1. In a medium saucepan, combine cornstarch and 2½ cups cold water. Stir until smooth and free of lumps.

2. While stirring constantly, cook over medium heat until mixture begins to boil.

3. Remove from heat and stir in the remaining cold water and glycerine. Cool mixture about 10 minutes in pan.

4. Divide mixture into small jars and add a different color squirt of liquid tempera paint to each jar. Stir each jar until thoroughly mixed.

5. Use *Finger Paint* on any kind of paper, but shiny thick paper is best. Cover work surface with newspaper and put on an old shirt to protect your clothing.

Store unused Finger Paint, with lids securely in place, in a cool dark place.

Helping Hands

Finger Painting Gift Baskets for your friends let them be creative <u>and</u> get gooey at the same time. Put some shredded paper in the bottom of a basket, fill it with 3 or 4 jars of Finger Paint, some rolled up recycled paper and a smock. Copy the Finger Paint recipe on a gift card and attach it to the basket handle with curling ribbon. Violà! Your friends will love it!

DOG BISCUITS

TOOLS:
measuring cups
2 medium bowls
fork and rolling pin
cookie cutters or knife
non-stick spray cooking oil
cookie sheet

INGREDIENTS:
1 cup all-purpose flour
½ cup whole wheat flour
½ cup bran cereal
½ cup dry rolled oats
1 egg
½ cup 2% lowfat milk
¼ cup oil
¼ cup chicken broth

Preheat oven to 350°.

1. Combine all dry ingredients in one bowl. In a separate bowl, mix remaining ingredients with a fork.

2. Add liquid mixture to dry mixture and stir with a fork. Finish mixing with your hands until a dough forms.

3. Roll out dough on a lightly floured surface until it is ¼ inch thick.

4. Cut biscuits into shapes with cookie cutters, or use a butter knife to cut dog bone shapes. Place on a cookie sheet that has been sprayed with non-stick cooking oil. Bake 12 minutes, then turn off oven and let the biscuits harden overnight in the oven.

Your dog will do flips for these!
Store in an airtight container.

Animal Fact
There are thousands of dogs and cats in animal shelters waiting for good homes. Neutering or spaying pets prevents them from reproducing, and reduces the number of homeless animals.

CAT'S MEOW

Cats love to munch on this treat, and it's good for them, too!

TOOLS:
small plastic dish with lid
(like a soft margarine tub)

INGREDIENTS:
garden soil
1 tablespoon grass seed

1. Poke holes in the bottom of the plastic dish with a fork.

2. Fill plastic dish half full of garden soil, smooth to level. Sprinkle grass seed over soil, followed by just a little more soil, then sprinkle with water.

3. Place dish upside down on plastic lid and put in a sunny spot. Keep moist, but not too wet, until grass sprouts. Keep dish where your cat can reach it for snacking. Water when soil is dry.

BIRD TREATS

TOOLS:
small bowl
measuring cups
plastic mesh onion bag

INGREDIENTS:
½ cup cornmeal
½ cup peanut butter
¼ cup sunflower seeds
¼ cup raisins

1. Combine all ingredients and form into a ball. Chill 30 minutes to firm.

2. Place in mesh bag, or spread on a pinecone. Hang on a tree branch.

HEAP O' COMPOST

TOOLS:

4 wooden planks (8" x 4')
4 wooden stakes (5' long)
hammer or rubber mallet
18 feet of chicken wire
 (4' wide)
16 "U"-shaped nails or tacks
2 pieces of strong but
 flexible wire (1' long)
4'x4' carpet remnant or tarp

INGREDIENTS:

organic matter from the
yard and garden (leaves,
 cut grass, sticks, twigs)
organic matter from the
kitchen (veggie peelings,
tea leaves, leftovers,
 but NO MEAT SCRAPS)
manure or nitrogen activator
 (from a garden center)
soil and water

*Compost will be ready in 5 months.
Shovel onto plants to add
nutrients to help your
garden grow.*

1. Find a location near your garden and away from houses that is 4' x 4'.

2. Lay wooden planks to form a platform. Leave a 6-inch space between planks for air to circulate.

3. At each corner of the 4' x 4' area, drive a wooden stake about 1 foot deep into the ground.

4. Use a hammer and "U"-shaped nails or tacks to attach one end of chicken wire to the stake nearest your garden. Wrap chicken wire around area, attaching it to the other 3 stakes.

5. Twist a piece of wire through the top of the chicken wire attached to the first stake. Twist the other wire through the bottom of the chicken wire attached to first stake. Use these wires to hold the loose segment of chicken wire, the "door," you can swing open to shovel out the compost.

6. In the compost pit, start with a layer of sticks and twigs. Now begin alternating layers of leaves and grass, organic kitchen matter, nitrogen activator, soil and water. Cover with carpet remnant and keep it moist. Continue adding layers as you accumulate kitchen waste.

Helping Hands

A small dry "sleeping" seed might seem insignificant, but give it good soil, water and sunshine and watch it awaken! It is surprising how many vegetables can grow in a small plot, or even in patio containers. Choose a location that receives the most sunlight each day. Measure the space and draw a plan to decide where each plant will grow. Some plants need special placement or a lot of room. For example, sunflowers block the sun from other plants, so they should be planted in the rear (the north or west side). Check the seed packets for spacing distances. Prepare the soil by loosening it with a shovel, breaking up clumps, and mixing in organic matter such as compost or peat moss. Plant seeds according to instructions on the packet and water well. Once your seeds have sprouted and several are a couple of inches tall, you can put more organic matter around them. This keeps in moisture, fertilizes the plants and helps control weed growth. Water the garden in the evenings when dry, and pull weeds to give vegetables room to grow. Soon you'll be picking your homegrown produce!

MAKE YOUR OWN RECYCLED PAPER

Start the day before, for an outdoor summertime get-wet project!
Select an out-of-the-way area where you can leave the paper to dry.

TOOLS:

4-gallon bucket
long-handled wooden spoon
9" x 13" x 2"-deep pan
8"-square piece wire mesh
   (from hardware store)
   with narrow masking
   tape folded around edges
old towels and blankets cut
   into 24 squares of
   12" x 12" or larger
plastic bag
books or flat heavy objects
newspaper or paper bags

INGREDIENTS:

2-3 lbs. newspaper (no fliers,
   cardboard or inserts)
lots of water

* Make your paper extra fancy by
stirring small soft leaves
and flower petals into the pulp
before scooping it onto the mesh.

1. Rip newspaper into small pieces. Soak overnight in a bucket of water.

2. The next day, pour out most of the water, leaving a couple of inches of water in the bucket. Use a wooden spoon to mash paper and water into a pulp.

3. Scoop 2 cups of pulp into the pan. Add 2 cups water and stir well. *

4. Slide the wire mesh under the pulp mixture. Lift it out covered in pulp.

5. Lay a cloth square on a hard smooth surface. Quickly flip the pulp over onto the cloth. Press down over the surface of the mesh, then slowly peel the mesh back, leaving pulp on the cloth. Press another cloth on top to absorb moisture, and leave it in place.

6. Continue mixing equal amounts of pulp and water in the pan, scooping out with the mesh, and making alternate layers of pulp and cloth.

7. Place a plastic bag on the top, and weight down the pile with books. Wait at least 6 hours for the pulp to turn into paper. Gently peel the paper from the cloths. Lay your paper out to dry on newspaper or paper bags.

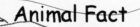

Animal Fact

There are two kinds of elephants: African elephants and Asiatic (or Indian) elephants. It is easy to tell them apart, African elephants have huge Dumbo-sized ears and backs that curve down in the middle. Asiatic elephants have smaller ears and backs that curve up in the middle. Elephants are the largest of all land mammals. At birth, a newborn elephant calf is about 3 feet tall and weighs about 200 pounds. Most adult males are 9-10 feet tall and weigh over 10,000 pounds! Not only are elephants huge, they have HUGE appetites. Adult elephants eat up to 300 pounds of food and drink 42 gallons of water per day! Most of a wild elephant's diet consists of grasses. But, they also eat about 100 other kinds of food including tree bark, leaves and fruit. Elephants are very social. The females and young elephants stay together in groups, called herds. Within a herd, the elephants are usually friendly to each other. They often nuzzle each other to show affection, and all females in the herd protect and nurture the calves.

VEGGIE OIL DYE STATIONERY

This exquisite marbled paper is a work of art in itself!

TOOLS:

newspaper

large mixing bowl

measuring spoons

rubber mallet

1 custard cup or small bowl
   for each color dye

fork

lots of paper bags

INGREDIENTS:

water

2 tablespoons vinegar

1 tablespoon vegetable oil
   for each color of dye

colored chalk

half sheets of white paper

1. Lay a few sheets of newspaper on counter or tabletop. Place mixing bowl on newspaper and fill to the top with water. Add vinegar to water.

2. Break one color of chalk into small pieces and place between two pieces of newspaper. Gently crush into a powder with the mallet. Pour powdered chalk into a custard cup or small bowl. Stir in 1 tablespoon of vegetable oil. Repeat process for each color of chalk.

3. Pour a few colorful drops from each cup into the mixing bowl. Swirl around just once with your finger.

4. Place a sheet of paper on the water's surface for just 1 second, then lift away. Lay sheet on flattened paper bag to dry for 24 hours. Repeat steps 3 and 4 for each sheet of paper.

5. When paper is completely dry, gently wipe off any surface chalk grains with a clean dry cloth.

Helping Hands

Make an "I Promise to Write Kit" for yourself or a gift. Take a pocket folder and put in some homemade stationery, envelopes, a pen or pencil, some stickers and maybe a few postage stamps. Draw a picture on the front and write addresses on the inside front of the pockets.

Ecology Fact

Life in the oceans is as varied as life on land. Fish, marine mammals, seabirds and fishermen all depend on a healthy unpolluted ocean for their existence. Oil tankers move millions of tons of oil around the world each year. When an oil tanker has an accident, oil can spill into the sea. The oil collects on the surface of the water in large pools. Sea birds and otters are just two of the many animals that are in severe danger from oil spills. Birds' feathers have little barbs or hooks that keep the individual feathers together, and the wind and water out. Oil causes the feathers to separate, making it difficult for the bird to fly or stay warm. Like the sea birds' feathers, the fur of the sea otter keeps it warm because it keeps wind and water out. When oil gets on a sea otter, its fur is flattened and unable to keep it warm and dry. New legislation that makes oil tanker companies accountable for their actions is helping protect the sea and the many lives that depend on it.

HOMEMADE GLUE

TOOLS:
measuring cups and spoons
2 small paper drinking cups
mixing spoon
cheesecloth to use as filter

INGREDIENTS:
¼ cup milk
1 tablespoon white vinegar
pinch baking soda

1. Pour the milk into one of the cups. Add the vinegar and stir for 1 minute. The mixture will form clumps (curds) and clear liquid (whey).

2. Place the cheesecloth over the second cup and push the middle down a bit.

3. Holding the cheesecloth in place, slowly pour the curds and whey into the cloth. Most of the whey will flow through the cloth into the cup. Gently squeeze the rest of the whey into the cup, then throw the liquid whey away.

4. Scrape the curds into the empty cup. Add the baking soda and stir well. You now have glue!

This is a good glue for paper projects. Allow a couple of hours for it to dry.

Helping Hands

Put some glue in a small squeeze bottle or old glue bottle, then mix in a little food coloring or tempera paint. Use the colored glue to draw pictures or add 3-D accents to artwork. Glue is thicker than paint so allow extra time for it to dry.

HOMEMADE GLUE II

TOOLS:
measuring cups and spoons
small saucepan
wooden spoon
small jar with tight lid

INGREDIENTS:
½ cup cornstarch
2 tablespoons sugar
1 cup cold water

1. In a small saucepan, stir together cornstarch and sugar.

2. Add cold water and stir until cornstarch and sugar are dissolved.

3. Stirring constantly, cook over medium heat until paste forms.

Store in a small tightly sealed jar.

Animal Fact

Koalas are near the top of everybody's list of the world's cutest animals. With their sleepy friendly faces and tufts of fur surrounding their ears, they are incredibly adorable. Most people think of Koalas as bears, but Koalas are not even closely related to bears. Instead, Koalas belong to a group of animals called marsupials. Like other marsupials (and unlike bears), Koalas have pouches for carrying their babies. To see Koalas in their natural habitat, you would have to visit Australia where the eucalyptus trees grow. Koalas are very picky eaters and only eat the leaves of the eucalyptus tree. Even then, of the over 600 kinds of eucalyptus trees, some Koalas will eat only two or three kinds of eucalyptus. Their large nose helps them decide what to eat, and the Koala sniffs every leaf to be sure it is fit to eat. Koalas are nocturnal animals, sleeping during the day and wide awake and eating through the night. The biggest threat to Koalas is loss of their habitat. Australia has begun preserving eucalyptus groves to ensure the future of this sweet looking animal.

TIE-DYED SOCKS

TOOLS:
small saucepan
wooden spoon
pie tin
rubber bands
white socks
rubber gloves

INGREDIENTS:
1 package colorful flavored
   powdered drink mix
¼ cup vinegar
1¾ cups water

1. In a small saucepan, stir together all ingredients until well blended.

2. Place saucepan over medium-high heat. Stirring constantly, bring mixture to a boil for 1 minute.

3. Remove from heat and let cool.

4. While dye mixture is cooling, pinch pieces of the socks and twist. Wrap a rubber band tightly around each pinched piece. (The dye won't reach the places that are tightly bound.)

5. When the dye mixture has completely cooled, dip the bound socks into the dye for 30 seconds.

6. Lightly squeeze excess moisture from socks and hang to dry. (If desired, repeat process for more colors before drying.) When socks are almost dry, remove rubber bands and hang to finish drying.

Seriously funky socks!

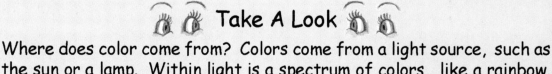

Take A Look

Where does color come from? Colors come from a light source, such as the sun or a lamp. Within light is a spectrum of colors, like a rainbow. Everything we see as having color contains pigments that absorb some colors in the light, and reflect other colors back to our eyes. A red rose looks red because it absorbs every color but red, so only red light is reflected back to our eyes. Without light there is no color!

Ecology Fact

Rain forests are home to at least three-quarters of the Earth's wildlife. Millions of plant and animal species live there, and new species are being discovered every day. Many medicines are made from plants that grow only in the rain forest, and scientists are sure many more cures will be found from these species. The rain forests also play a vital role in regulating the world's climate through the oxygen, carbon and water cycles. In the communities next to the rain forests, increasing human population and impoverished conditions cause people to cut rain forest trees for building materials and to create farmland. Rich nations also demand these timbers for furniture, paper and construction projects. Almost half of the world's rain forests have already been destroyed. You can help by recycling newspapers, cardboard and product packaging, and not wasting paper. Please remember never to buy furniture made from rain forest trees, such as teak and mahogany.

143

MAGIC MUD

Few things are as fun as playing in the mud!

TOOLS:
9" × 9" × 2"-deep pan
measuring cups and spoons

INGREDIENTS:
2 cups cornstarch
1 cup cold water
1 tablespoon food coloring

Helping Hands

Make your own environmentally friendly cleaning products that work great, too!

Super Window Shiner:
    ¼ cup white vinegar
    1 quart water

Wood Cleaner and Polisher:
    2 tablespoons olive oil
    2 tablespoons white vinegar
    1 quart water

Terrific Tub and Tile Cleaner:
    3 tablespoons baking soda
    1 quart warm water

Used fabric-softener sheets make great dust cloths. The dust clings to the softening-agent residue.

1. Combine cornstarch, water and food coloring in the pan.

2. Mix mud with your hands until completely smooth.

Is it a liquid or a solid? Check it out...

...Scoop up a handful of *Magic Mud* and squeeze it in your hand. Now open up your hand...YUK!

...Slap the *Magic Mud* with the palm of your hand.

...Now gently push your hand around in it.

When you squeeze it or slap it quickly, it becomes hard. But when you move it around or push it slowly, it acts like a liquid. This is because cornstarch is ground into such fine particles that the molecules line up like little plates. The plates stay rigid when squeezed or slapped, but slide around when released and there is little or no pressure.

Store in an airtight container. Magic Mud can be kept for several days; just add a little water if it dries out.

Animal Fact

The ancient Greeks named the large African water mammal "hippopotamus" which means "river horse." Hippos come in two varieties. The small pygmy hippo lives in rain forests and swamps, and the gigantic common hippo is usually found in rivers and lakes. Hippos are awkward on land but glide through the water in a graceful slow-motion ballet. In fact, common hippos spend most of their time in the water, only coming out at night to eat. They nap in shallow water or mudholes most of the day and slowly trudge onto land at dusk to eat. The ears, eyes and nostrils of the common hippo are all on top of its huge head. This lets the animal hear, see and breathe at the surface of the water while the rest of its body is safely hidden underwater. A mother hippo looks after her own baby plus several others at a time. She is very strict about keeping them in a single-file line behind her. If any babies wander away or play while in line, she nudges or nips at them to get them back into position. This marvelous animal needs us to ensure the preservation of its habitat.

FRESH WATER MAKER

This project needs an adult's help and supervision, the steam is very hot!

TOOLS:
measuring cups and spoons
small saucepan with lid
oven mitts
glass or cup

INGREDIENTS:
2½ cups water and
1 tablespoon salt
   or
2½ cups unpolluted sea
   water if clean ocean
   water is nearby

1. In the small saucepan, combine water and salt, or pour in the sea water. Stir until the salt is dissolved. Taste the water now, it is very salty!

2. Turn the stove burner to medium-high until the water boils. Cover and turn the heat down to low. Simmer for 3-5 minutes.

3. Use oven mitts to remove the lid (be sure to tip it away from your face, the steam is very hot). Hold the lid over the cup and tip the lid so that the water that has collected on the underside of the lid drips into the cup. Keep doing this every few minutes until you have enough water to taste.

Taste the water in the cup. It tastes very similar to fresh water. What happened? As water heats it evaporates. The salt minerals in the water are too heavy to be lifted in the vapor, so most of the salt minerals stay behind. As the water vapor condenses on the lid without the salt, the condensation is less salty than the original water. Not only is the condensed water purified, but most harmful bacteria have also been killed by boiling.

This process is similar to a process ships use at sea to transform salt water to fresh water.

Ecology Fact

How much do you contribute to the world's water pollution? More than half of U.S. water pollution begins as runoff from city streets, construction sites, farms, etc. Fertilizers and pesticides applied to lawns and gardens are often washed off by rain, and concentrate in nearby lakes at levels high enough to kill aquatic life. To prevent this from happening, never pour toxic chemicals down the drain or on the ground. Landscape the yard with disease and pest resistant plants native to your area (they need less water, fertilizer and pesticides). Test the soil before applying fertilizers, so you use no more than necessary. Selecting porous materials, such as gravel, for walkways and driveways increases water filtration and decreases surface run-off. And finally, clean up after pets. Placing wastes in proper trash receptacles avoids runoff of nutrients and pathogens into surface waters. Did you know you could do so much to prevent water pollution?

ACID RAIN TEST DIP STICKS

TOOLS:
measuring cups
knife and cutting board
medium saucepan
strainer
cotton swabs
jar or large bowl
newspaper or paper towels

INGREDIENTS:
1 small head red cabbage
2 cups water

A small amount of these
   testing solutions:
rain water
garden soil mixed in water
lemon juice
vinegar
wood ashes mixed in water
baking soda mixed in water
saliva
tomato juice
sea water

1. Cut cabbage up into small pieces and put in saucepan with the 2 cups of water. Bring to a boil over medium-high heat. Reduce heat to low, simmer 5 minutes.

2. Remove from heat and cool completely. Drain water through strainer into a large jar or bowl. (Use the boiled cabbage for a side dish.)

3. Dip both ends of the cotton swabs into the cabbage water and lay them on a newspaper to dry.

4. When the swabs are dry, they are ready to be used as dip sticks. Dip sticks determine if a substance is an acid or a base by chemical reaction. Acids will turn the dip stick red. Bases will turn the dip stick blue.

5. Dip a fresh dip stick into each of the testing solutions to determine if it is an acid or a base. Record and compare your results.

You can use other vegetable and fruit juices instead of red cabbage juice. Try making dip sticks with boiled beet or blueberry juice.

Ecology Fact

Acid rain is created from gases released by the burning of coal and oil for fuel, as from factories and road vehicles. These gases react with sunlight and air moisture to produce rain with a high ph level, which is called "acidic" or acid rain. The effects of acid rain can be very serious. It changes the chemical component levels in soil, causing trees to lose their leaves and die. The corrosive rain even eats away at the features of statues. Lakes, rivers and streams are most affected by acid rain and can become too acidic for aquatic life to live in. Where the problem is most severe, lime is dumped into the water body to neutralize the acid. To help reduce acid rain, conserve the use of energy: Turn off lights, minimize heating and air conditioning, and walk, bike or carpool whenever possible.

RUBBER EGG

TOOLS:
measuring cups
small glass jar
   (baby-food jar size)

INGREDIENTS:
1 egg (in shell)
¾ cup vinegar

1. Place the egg in the jar and cover with vinegar.

2. Check the egg frequently over the next several hours. The hard eggshell disappears, leaving a rubbery egg sac surrounding the white and yolk.

What happened? Vinegar is an acid which thins and weakens the egg's shell until it eventually turns into a flexible and rubbery egg sac. This process is similar to the effect the chemical DDT had on bald eagle eggs.

Ecology Fact

When DDT was first developed it worked so well that it was considered the "miracle pesticide." But in the 1950's, it became apparent that DDT and its related compounds were not easily broken down in the environment. The use of the pesticide almost wiped out the American bald eagle population, and it reduced the populations of many other birds as well. DDT created a calcium imbalance in the adult birds, causing females to lay eggs with such thin shells that they tended to break during incubation. Despite this information, the use of DDT continued through the 1970's until it was banned in the U.S. and most other countries. Like DDT, many other pesticides have also been banned. The American bald eagle and other bird populations are stable once again. Please support government actions that encourage the use of safe pest control methods worldwide.

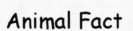

Animal Fact

Have you ever looked up in wonder at a bird soaring high above in the sky? People are fascinated by birds. The majesty of an eagle is a sight to behold. With their huge wingspan, eagles glide silently through the sky. They are also top predators and have a keen vision made for hunting. All eagles can see small objects up to two miles away. Their bodies are light enough to fly high in the air, but strong enough to swoop down on prey and carry it away. Eagles catch fish, small mammals and other birds. Although it might be upsetting to think of eagles hunting other animals, they are just doing their part to keep the world in balance. If it weren't for predators, such as the eagle, the numbers of other animals would get out of hand. Soon there would be too many animals and not enough food for their survival. Eagles are so good at catching food that they have plenty of time for fun. One game they play is to carry a stick high into the air and drop it. Then, they swoop down and catch it in midair before it hits the ground. What a bird!

GLOSSARY

Bake   To cook in an oven with hot dry air.

Beat   To repeatedly mix hard with a spoon, fork, whisk, beater or electric mixer.

Blend   To mix ingredients until smooth.

Boil   To heat liquid until bubbles break on the surface.

Chill   To refrigerate until cold.

Chop   To cut into bite-sized pieces with a knife.

Cool   To let hot food sit at room temperature until it is no longer hot.

Cream   To beat until soft and creamy, as when mixing butter and sugar.

Cube   To cut into ¼-½-inch squares.

Dice   To chop into small pieces. (Finely Dice: Chop into very small pieces.)

Flour   To dust lightly with flour. To flour a greased pan, coat the bottom and sides lightly and shake off excess flour that fails to stick.

Grate   To shred into small bits by rubbing against a grater, or by processing in a food processor.

Grease   To rub a dish or pan with butter, margarine, oil or shortening so that food does not stick.

Knead   To work dough with your hands until it becomes smooth and stretchy. Kneading is done on a floured surface by pressing and pushing dough away from you, turning it and repeating the process.

Mix   To stir together two or more ingredients.

Peel   To remove skins from citrus fruits, bananas and vegetables with a knife, or by pulling them off with your fingers.

Preheat   To heat an oven to a certain temperature before using. Most ovens take about 10 minutes to preheat.

Sauté   To cook briefly in a small amount of fat or water in a fry pan or skillet. The food should be stirred or turned often.

Sift   To put flour or other powdery ingredient through a fine mesh or sifter to make it lighter and remove lumps. Sifted flour will measure less than unsifted flour.

Simmer   To cook a liquid that is almost boiling, but not bubbling. The surface of a simmering liquid usually has some slight movement.

Stir   To mix round and round with a spoon or fork.

Whip   To beat with a whisk, electric mixer or egg beater. Eggs and heavy cream become thick and fluffy as air is beaten into them.

152

MEASUREMENT CONVERSION TABLE

Measurement Equivalents	1 tablespoon	1/4 cup	1/2 cup	1/3 cup	1 cup	1 pint	1 quart	1 gallon	1 fluid oz.	1 pound
3 teaspoons	●									
2 tablespoons									●	
4 tablespoons		●								
8 tablespoons			●							
5 tablespoons + 1 teaspoon				●						
16 tablespoons					●					
2 cups						●				
4 cups							●			
8 fluid ounces					●					
16 fluid ounces						●				
32 fluid ounces							●			
½ pint					●					
2 pints							●			
4 quarts								●		
1 stick butter		●								
2¼ cups sugar										●
4 cups flour										●

153

EATING & LIVING SMART

Each recipe has a nutritional analysis indicating the nutritional values within each serving. Use this information to make sure you are eating the nutrients necessary for good health. The Recommended Daily Intake (RDI) shown for each item has been determined by the American Dietetic Association for ages 7 to 14. Children's vitamins can also help you reach the Recommended Daily Intake ("RDI") of vitamins and nutrients.

Calories: For energy. RDI: 2,000-2,500 calories

Protein: For cell and muscle growth. RDI: 28-45 gm

Fat: Energy reserve; needed for brain development. RDI: 66-83 gm

Carbohydrates (Carbs): Fuel for activity. RDI: 250-312 gm

Calcium: For strong bones and teeth. RDI: 800-1,200 mg

Sodium: Limit to prevent chronic diseases. RDI: Not to exceed 2,400 mg

Cholesterol: Limit to prevent heart disease. RDI: Not to exceed 300 mg

To be healthy people, we need proper diet and exercise. Exercise every day in organized sports, walking, hiking, biking or swimming. Eat a wide variety of foods in proper amounts for the nutrients you need. Try to eat whole foods closest to their original form, such as fresh fruits and vegetables. Limit fat intake (like greasy burgers and french fries) and go for foods rich in carbohydrates, such as cereals, grains, fruits and vegetables.

Life choices can also help preserve the health of the Earth. Negative effects on the environment developed over many years, and reversing those trends will take time. Like following a recipe, this is accomplished by taking one simple step followed by the next. Make it a habit to pick up litter on the street, recycle used materials and conserve energy. Select store-bought products with less packaging and those that use recycled materials. Learn as much as you can. Be involved! Kids can be the most important voice in making change happen. Tell your teachers, parents and scout or youth group leaders what you'd like to do, and ask them for their help in organizing a project to improve your world.

Eating and living smart is a matter of personal responsibility.
The power of your choices is greater than you think.
Make the world a better place because you are here!

FOR MORE INFORMATION

If you would like to know more, here are some addresses of conservation groups. Some work to maintain and improve habitats for animals and plants. Other organizations focus on education and work to influence business, public opinion or government legislation. Write for information and ask if they have children's groups or activity packets (include a stamped, self-addressed envelope for their reply). Check with your school, church, scouting and youth groups for programs to help protect the Earth and wildlife.

* The Nature Conservancy
1815 North Lynn Street
Arlington, VA 22209
Preserves habitat for endangered species. Programs for kids include Rescue the Reef, Adopt an Acre, and Adopt a Bison.

Friends of the Earth (FOE)
218 D Street, SE
Washington, D.C. 20003
Promotes understanding and appreciation of the need for preservation of natural resources.

World Wildlife Fund
1250 Twenty-fourth Street, NW
Washington, D.C. 20037-1175
Works to preserve the diversity and abundance of life on Earth and the health of ecological systems.

National Wildlife Federation
1400 Sixteenth Street, NW
Washington, D.C. 20036-2266
Educational efforts help to conserve wildlife and natural resources.

Sierra Club
730 Polk Street
San Francisco, CA 94109
Encourages exploration and protection of the Earth's wild places through education and nature outings.

Rain Forest Alliance
270 Lafayette St., Suite 512
New York, NY 10012
Works to save tropical rain forests around the world.

The Cousteau Society
930 W. 21st Street
Norfolk, VA 23517
Seeks the conservation of natural resources and protection of the environment through research and education.

EarthSave
600 Distillery Commons, Suite 200
Louisville, KY 40206
Educates people on the impact food choices have on the environment, and the benefits of a plant-based diet.

* In support of global awareness, the publisher of this book, Harvest Hill Press, donates $1,000 per year to The Nature Conservancy, and is a Corporate Associate of The Nature Conservancy.

RECIPE INDEX

RECIPE INDEX

FACTOID INDEX

158

NOTES

To order more copies of

HEY KIDS!
You're Cookin' Now!
A Global Awareness Cooking Adventure

Photocopy this page or send a note with the requested information.

Your Name _____

Street Address _____

City, State, Zip _____

Daytime Telephone _____

For shipment to another address, shall we enclose a gift tag?_____

Ship-to Name _____

Street Address _____

City, State, Zip _____

Cost per Book	$ 19.95
Number of Books	x _____
Sub-Total Cost	$ _____
Shipping at $3.05 /book	$ _____
Maine Residents Only	$ _____ - Add $1.10 sales tax per book
Total Enclosed	$ _____ - Check or VISA/M.C. below

VISA/M.C. Cardholder's Printed Name_____

VISA/M.C. Cardholder's Signature _____

VISA/M.C. # _____ Expiration _____

Mail with your check or credit card information to:
Harvest Hill Press, P.O.Box 55, Salisbury Cove, Maine 04672
or call 207-288-8900

THANK YOU FOR THIS ORDER!